ANOTHER KIND OF COWBOY

ALSO BY
Susan Juby

Alice, I Think

Miss Smithers

Alice MacLeod, Realist at Last

ANOTHER KIND OF COWBOY

Susan Juby

HARPER TEEN

An Imprint of HarperCollins*Publishers*

HarperTeen is an imprint of HarperCollins Publishers.

Another Kind of Cowboy
Copyright © 2007 by Susan Juby
www.harperteen.com

Library of Congress Cataloging-in-Publication Data
Juby, Susan, 1969-
    Another kind of cowboy / by Susan Juby. — 1st ed.
        p.   cm.
    Summary: In Vancouver, British Columbia, two teenage
dressage riders, one a spoiled rich girl and the other a closeted
gay sixteen-year-old boy, come to terms with their identities and
learn to accept themselves.
    ISBN 978-0-06-076517-0 (trade bdg.)
    ISBN 978-0-06-076518-7 (lib. bdg.)
    [1. Dressage—Fiction. 2. Horsemanship—Fiction. 3. Horses—
Fiction. 4. Homosexuality—Fiction. 5. Family life—British
Columbia—Fiction. 6. British Columbia—Fiction.] I. Title.
PZ7.J858Ano 2007   2006036336
[Fic]—dc22   CIP
                                                              AC

Typography by Amy Ryan
1 2 3 4 5 6 7 8 9 10
❖
First Edition

HarperTeen is an imprint of HarperCollins Publishers.

Another Kind of Cowboy
Copyright © 2007 by Susan Juby

www.harperteen.com

Library of Congress Cataloging-in-Publication Data
Juby, Susan, 1969-
  Another kind of cowboy / by Susan Juby. — 1st ed.
    p. cm.
  Summary: In Vancouver, British Columbia, two teenage
dressage riders, one a spoiled rich girl and the other a closeted
gay sixteen-year-old boy, come to terms with their identities and
learn to accept themselves.
  ISBN 978-0-06-076517-0 (trade bdg.)
  ISBN 978-0-06-076518-7 (lib. bdg.)
  [1. Dressage—Fiction. 2. Horsemanship—Fiction. 3. Horses—
Fiction. 4. Homosexuality—Fiction. 5. Family life—British
Columbia—Fiction. 6. British Columbia—Fiction.] I. Title.
PZ7.J858Ano 2007   2006036336
[Fic]—dc22   CIP
                                        AC

Typography by Amy Ryan
1 2 3 4 5 6 7 8 9 10
❖
First Edition

ANOTHER KIND OF COWBOY

Susan Juby

HARPER TEEN

An Imprint of HarperCollins*Publishers*

FOR MY MOTHER, who sacrificed to make riding possible when I was a kid, and for my husband, James, who graciously tolerates the obsession I continue to nurture.

The greatest difficulty in equitation is to keep the horse straight.

— *The Manual of Horsemanship*

In the beginning . . .

THERE WAS DEL Magnifico le Noir. If you didn't know better, you might have mistaken him for a dark-blue Norco bike, but to six-year-old Alex Ford, Magnifico was a three-year-old Thoroughbred, reminiscent of the Black Stallion. Like the Black Stallion, Magnifico was given to bursts of thrilling speed, which is why Alex kept a red dog leash tied to his handlebars.

Alex rode Magnifico around his rural neighborhood, whispering "whoa" at stop signs and using an assortment of what he imagined were horsey noises, such as clucks and peculiar trills, to urge the bike through puddles and over small obstacles. Using a Pony Club–approved slip knot, he tied Magnifico outside the school each day and each night brought the bike into the garage for a brisk rubdown, and covered it with an old blanket, fastened with a leatherlike belt he'd taken from one of his mother's old pantsuits. Alex kept a dog dish filled with water in front of the bike and hung an aluminum fishnet full of dried grass clippings just over Magnifico's handlebars.

Once, when Alex's teenage cousins were visiting, they stole Magnifico and rode him to the store to purchase cheese-flavored snacks. Upon their return, they left the bike on the lawn. When Alex found Magnifico lying in the rain, his deflated front tire spinning helplessly, his red leash muddy and sodden, Alex burst into tears. This was just like the time when the drunken stableman ruined Black Beauty's knees by galloping him with a rock in his shoe.

Slowly, Alex pushed Magnifico into the garage where he inflated his tire and then walked him in circles for over an hour. When he was sure Magnifico was going to live, he made him a hot bran mash, wrapped him in extra blankets, and vowed fervently that he'd never let anything like that happen to him again. To their credit, Alex's cousins felt alarmed and guilty at Alex's dramatic reaction. They even brought the bike an apple to make up for what they'd done.

Sometimes Alex felt as if he was set apart from other people. It wasn't just that he was secretly a naturally gifted horseman with a bike called Del Magnifico le Noir. He suspected he was different in other ways, too, though he couldn't have said how. Thinking about it made him uncomfortable, so he didn't. Instead, he tended to Magnifico and immersed himself in horse novels and reference books. He diligently committed to memory *The Complete Encyclopedia of Horses* and *Horse Husbandry: A Compendium*. He took the two giant reference volumes out from the library over and over again until the librarian, who had noticed Magnifico wasn't actually a horse, told him he had to "give them a break because someone else in the neighborhood might want to know something about looking after their bikes." Alex just blinked owlishly.

Fortunately, soon after the librarian cut him off from the reference books, Alex discovered horses on television. He was awed by the dashing horse-and-rider teams who careened around the courses and flew over looming jumps. In no time he'd learned the names of all the top show jumpers on ESPN. Alex wasn't simply watching the horses onscreen—he *was* the horses onscreen. His head jerked up and down as the horses cleared jumps and obstacles, and when one of them hit a pole or stumbled, he would develop a sympathy limp that could last as long as an hour.

Then one day Alex found a new horse sport on TV. The announcer called it "corsage." Alex was instantly mesmerized by the riders who wore top hats and tails and rode their massive horses in intricate patterns around a low-sided white ring. The horses didn't jump; instead they walked, pranced, and cantered, forward and sideways, in circles and across the diagonals. At times they trotted in place, and at other times they flung out their legs so far they seemed almost to fly. All the while their riders sat perfectly still and elegant.

This corsage riding was astonishing to Alex—it was like dancing with your horse!

At the first commercial break Alex nearly levitated off the couch. With his back straight, his hands held elegantly in front of him, he pranced across the room. He cantered a few steps forward, then sideways. Imaginary music swirled in his head. When the commercials ended, he rushed back to the couch to continue watching.

Alex was in love with the horses. He was in love

with the riders. But most of all, he was profoundly in love with corsage. He watched the rest of the competition in a state of barely suppressed exultation. The names of the movements called out by the announcer—piaffe, passage, pirouette—were all so . . . so . . . French! Even the word *corsage* appealed to him. When the program ended, Alex was on his feet again, passaging boldly around the living room. He rolled his shoulders, lifting his knees as high as they'd go, until his father came to the doorway and broke the spell by calling out, "Jesus, Darlene, how much sugar has he had today?"

Alex ignored his father and swept past him to the garage, where he put on Magnifico's best seat cover and rode up and down the driveway as elegantly as he could. Alex knew exactly what he'd do when he finally got his own horse. He was going to wear a top hat and tails and ride in a low-sided white ring, a massive crowd cheering in the stands and beautiful music all around him. He was going to become a corsage rider and he was going to dance with horses.

His aunt Grace happened to be visiting that day and after she watched him ride Magnifico in a perfectly symmetrical figure eight she asked him what he was doing.

"Corsage," said Alex, stopping Magnifico by pulling on the handlebar leash and putting down his feet.

"Corsage?" said Grace.

"You know, that kind of riding people do in the white rings with the letters."

Grace kept her face very still. "I think you might mean dressage," she said. "Corsage is a kind of flower arrangement."

"Oh," said Alex. He stared down at Magnifico for a moment, then looked up at his aunt. "Really?"

"Absolutely. Let's see more dressage. I think you're doing some excellent work out here."

"Okay," said Alex, his face lighting up like someone had flipped a switch.

Unfortunately, Alex's parents didn't share his aunt's enthusiasm for his new passion. His parents had no sympathy for his horse-riding ambitions. In fact, his mother actively thwarted them. Whenever the subject was raised, she would wail that a horse would be the end of them—the absolute end.

"Dirty, filthy things," she'd say, her lipsticked mouth curling over shiny, bleached teeth. "We have nowhere to keep one. Do I look like a farm wife to you, Brian?" she demanded of her husband. "Well? Do I?"

Alex's father would shrug his big shoulders and sigh and send an apologetic glance in his son's direction.

Alex wasn't even allowed to go to horse camp. Every summer the twins, Maggie and May, went to martial arts camp. Instead of horse camp, Alex was sent to a dingy, overgrown Pentecostal Bible camp. The Ford family wasn't religious, but Bible camp was cheap and it was close. The low cost was achieved by feeding the campers a diet of pure reconstituted starch. Every summer Alex, a slight boy, nearly doubled in size. He came home looking nearly as pale as the other campers, as well as puffy and convinced he was going to burn in hell.

The summer he turned eleven, Alex was surprised when his father was the one who came to get him from camp.

Brian Ford was mostly noticeable around the house for his absence and his silence. His wife treated him like an annoying, barely functional household appliance. As a result, Brian Ford spent as much time each day as possible at Turnaround RV, the used RV sales center he owned, and his nights at the Wheat Sheaf Pub. He left his wife to reign over the house, a task she accomplished through elaborate personal grooming and questionable redecorating schemes. She mostly encouraged her three children to stay out of the way.

On the drive home from camp, Alex appreciated his father's attempts to make conversation but was uncertain how to respond. When his father asked, "Hey, Bud, how they hanging?" Alex offered him a wary glance and a tortured smile.

His father's questions about the vehicles Alex had seen around Bible camp fell similarly flat, at least until Alex remembered that Reverend Bill had a new vehicle, purchased, presumably, with money saved on vegetables and fruit.

"Reverend Bill's got a new car," he said.

"Yeah? What'd he get?"

Alex thought for a long moment. "A blue one?"

"Blue?"

Alex added desperately, "Yeah. I think it might have been one of those V-8s." He was under the mistaken impression that V-8 was one of the Big Three automakers.

"Well," said Mr. Ford, and he didn't ask another question for the rest of the ride home.

By the time the big black truck pulled into the

driveway Mr. Ford had perked up again.

"I think you'll be real glad to be home," he said.

Alex agreed. While inadequate in many ways, his home and family were a definite improvement over Bible camp.

When they got out of the truck, Alex's father reached into the bed of the pickup for Alex's duffel bag.

"Notice anything new around here, Bud?"

The house remained boxlike and vinyl-sided. The lawn was a chemically induced bright green. There was no garden.

"Uh, no?" Alex was beginning to suspect a trick.

"Sure?"

Alex jerked his head around again. Suddenly he noticed white tape fencing peeking out from behind the house.

"You put up a fence," he said.

"Why don't you go have a look."

Alex walked along the side of the house to the back. White fencing, suspended on thin metal posts, now enclosed the entire back of the property. As Alex cleared the edge of the back deck and walked past the trampoline, his heart contracted as though gripped by a giant hand. Standing among the stumps in the clear-cut pasture was a white horse with several large red patches and a long, shaggy mane.

Alex stood with his mouth hanging open, his gaze fixed hungrily upon the animal. The horse continued snatching at grass as though it hadn't eaten in a month.

"That's right, Bud. Got you a horse. His name's Colonel Turnipseed but that sounds kind of girly, so I think it's best if you just call him Turnip."

For a terrible moment Alex thought he was going to throw up. He'd hit excitement, passed through joy, and wound up nauseous. As he struggled to control himself he gradually became aware that his sisters and mother stood on the deck behind him. Maggie and May wore matching grins. The look on his mother's face was less enthusiastic.

"See, Brian? He doesn't even know what to do with the thing. I'm going to end up having to walk it and feed it," said Mrs. Ford.

"He knows," replied Mr. Ford. "Go ahead, Bud. The guy I got him from said he's real quiet."

"Dad won him from an old cowboy in a poker tournament," said Maggie.

"An ackaholic cowboy," added May, touchingly.

Mrs. Ford rolled her eyes.

Alex turned back to the horse and it lifted its head and looked right at him. Everything else faded away. Finally, Alex found his voice.

"Is there any tack?"

Mr. Ford looked confused.

"A halter and bridle and things?" explained Alex.

"Oh, yeah. The guy put all his stuff in the shed when he dropped him off yesterday. Nobody's touched him since."

Alex strode over to the green plastic garden shed and after rooting around for a moment in a tangle of equipment, extracted a threadbare nylon halter and a frayed rope, both of which were nearly white with age. He found the opening in the flimsy tape fence and slowly walked to the horse's shoulder.

Everyone fell silent.

Up close Alex could see that although the horse's belly was round, his ribs and hips were visible and his coat was covered in welts and bite marks.

"Hey, boy," said Alex.

The red-and-white horse turned its head and then sniffed at the hand Alex held out. Only fumbling a bit, Alex slipped the halter over the horse's head and carefully arranged the rope so it wasn't wrapped around his hand. The horse stood quietly at his side.

Finally Alex looked back toward the house, a huge smile illuminating his normally solemn face. His father and sisters beamed back at him. His mother was nowhere to be seen.

PHASE I

Riding the horse with a natural carriage on straight lines in the ordinary paces in free forward movement with the rein in contact and on a long rein. This is known as riding straight forward. This kind of riding may be practiced for itself alone.

—Alois Podhajsky, *The Complete Training of Horse and Rider in the Principles of Classical Horsemanship*

Alex Ford

MR. FORD LOVED having a cowboy for a son. Sometimes Alex thought his riding was the only thing his dad had left to live for. Alex realized almost as soon as he got Turnip that he would not be taking dressage lessons. The horse came with a Western saddle and bridle as well as some erratic notions about steering. Apparently the alcoholic cowboy who'd trained him had done a lot of drinking and riding.

After the first few spills, one of which left Alex unable to remember his own name for most of an afternoon, his father hired a local girl to give Alex Western riding lessons. Meredith, a young woman who trained quarter horses and paints, was almost supernaturally even-tempered and unflappable. She wore a uniform of braids and jeans and boots and looked seventeen, even though she was almost thirty.

Meredith taught Alex to ride and helped him retrain Turnip. "Getting his steering working," she called it. Turnip was not a handsome horse, but he was a remarkably willing and honest one. Meredith liked to say he had more try in him than any horse she'd ever known. In that way he was a good match for his owner, who'd changed from an imaginative child into a serious, hardworking, perpetually stressed young man who was only able to relax when he rode.

Other than their shared love of hard work, Alex and his horse were an odd match. Turnip was short, big eared, and roman nosed. He paddled when he trotted and his tail was as sparse as his mane was abundant. Alex, on the other hand, was tallish and well-proportioned. Most people who noticed him also noted that he was graceful, though perhaps not everyone knew to call it that. He was thrilled when people asked if he was from out of town and he treasured the memory of the time a visitor to Meredith's barn asked, "Who's the rich kid?" because of the careful way he carried himself.

The unlikeliness of their pairing must have

appealed to Meredith's sense of humor, because soon after she started teaching Alex, she began bringing him and Turnip to horse shows. That was five years ago. At first Alex and his horse received pitying glances, as though there was something a bit pathetic about the slightly shabby old paint groomed within an inch of his life and his poised young rider. When Alex overheard one woman joke that Turnip's blanket probably had cost more than the horse, Alex bit back a tart retort about her atrocious haircut. The smart green blanket *had* cost more than the poker hand that won his horse.

Meredith had Alex enter performance-based competitions only, like trail and Western riding and horsemanship, because she knew Turnip couldn't try his way out of ugliness and odd conformation. Under her tutelage, the odd couple, as Alex and his horse came to be known, became the pair to beat on Vancouver Island.

After nearly five years of winning, Alex suspected that if he asked Turnip to fly, the horse would probably give it his best shot. Alex loved competing and took great pride in his horse's accomplishments, but he still thought longingly about dressage. He was held back by the worry that asking Turnip to do dressage would be a bit like asking the old horse to fly. He also felt it would have been disloyal to leave Meredith to begin dressage training. Meredith was a first-rate horsewoman and the closest thing Alex had to a real friend.

Then there was the small matter of his father.

Alex's parents' marriage had begun to unravel soon after he got the horse. His mom announced she wanted a separation, and that she wanted his dad to move into a condominium in town. Instead, Mr. Ford purchased a recreational vehicle off his own sales lot and parked it in the driveway. He told anyone who asked that he wanted to stay close so he could keep an eye on the kids and on his wife's "gentlemen visitors." He must not have kept close enough watch, however, because a couple of years after he moved into his RV, his wife informed the family that her affair with a local insurance adjuster was serious and they were moving to Florida together. The adjuster, who had long sideburns and favored skinny ties and pointy shoes, was at least ten years younger than Alex's mother. She said he reminded her of Rod Stewart.

Now, four years after he'd moved out of the house, Mr. Ford's trailer was still parked alongside the house, and he was still living in it, even though his wife was long gone. He seemed to think that if he stayed very still and didn't change anything, she'd come back.

Alex didn't want to do anything to upset his father, who was in a precarious mental state, and switching from Western to dressage would definitely upset him. Mr. Ford never missed a horse show. He loved parading around in his expensive lizard-skin cowboy boots and tight blue jeans. He was always first into the beer garden at the shows and last out. Somehow, Alex couldn't see his dad getting the same kind of thrill out of hanging around dressage competitions.

Oh, but I would, thought Alex as he stood near the dressage rings at the Fall Fling Horse Show. At any mixed-discipline show Alex always found himself standing at the edge of the dressage rings. He loved looking at the horses in their neat braids. He admired the riders, almost all of whom were female, in their tidy breeches and velvet hats. But most of all he was fascinated by the dressage tests. There was something about the precision of it that appealed to him.

Today he stood against the wall of a judge's booth, tucked into the shade of the roof, his face hidden under the brim of his cowboy hat. When he turned to see who was up next he noticed a slender girl with bright blond hair tied in a neat bun at the nape of her neck standing just outside the warm-up ring. She held the reins of a huge horse in one hand and a pair of white leather gloves in the other. Alex was transfixed by the sight of the impossibly elegant girl and the gleaming, perfectly turned-out horse. The girl's white breeches and black jacket fit like they'd been custom-made. Her horse had to be nearly seventeen hands and seemed lit up from inside. The girl and her horse looked like an advertisement for gracious living.

Alex was so busy admiring them he was surprised when the girl turned her head slightly and stared right at him. At first he wasn't sure how to react, and he gave her what he hoped was a friendly smile. He'd fallen out of the smiling habit in the last few years. The girl looked away and he was flooded with embarrassment, standing there in his cowboy boots and big buckle, an unfamiliar smile sitting on his face like a fake moustache. The girl looked like she belonged in the pages of *Town and Country* and here he was, gawking at her.

Alex might be dressed like a cowboy but he didn't

feel totally comfortable in the role. Real cowboys dreamed of girls with big hair and tight jeans, bars with sawdust floors and cows and the open range. His dreams ran more to other cowboys as well as firemen, cops, and, for some reason he'd yet to figure out, paramedics. The less open range and the fewer cows, the better.

He realized that the girl, who had a pretty, fine-boned, inquisitive face, was staring at him again. Surprised, he nodded at her. In response, she turned and walked away.

Nicely played, Ford, he thought.

He was about to make his way over to the dressage ring to watch her ride, when he felt a hand on his shoulder. Then another one.

"Alex," said his sisters, speaking in unison. "You better come. It's Dad."

He turned to look at the twins, who wore black T-shirts and the short, wide-legged pants from their kung fu uniforms.

"When did you get here?" he asked.

"Grace picked us up from practice. Sorry we missed your classes. Did you win?"

"Of course he won," said Maggie. "He's related to us, isn't he? He's not some loser who doesn't win."

"Solid point," agreed May. "No one could argue with that logic."

Sometimes fourteen-year-old Maggie and May, with their shiny eyes and glossy brown hair, reminded Alex of otters. Their relentless playfulness had the effect of raising his spirits, no matter what else he was fretting about.

"I did okay," he said.

"Don't be like that," said May.

"Humility has no place in the personality of the elite athlete," said Maggie.

"Just ask Lance Armstrong," added May. "You'd never catch him being all humble like that."

Alex squinted at his sisters. *What were they talking about?* As usual, he had no idea.

"What's this about Dad?" he asked.

"He's plowed," said Maggie.

"Totally smashed," added May. "He's in the beer garden with some woman. Grace said you need to get him out of there before he ruins her chances with a vet student she's trying to pick up. She says he's about to open a large animal practice so he's ripe for either a relationship or a receptionist."

"Dad?"

"No, the vet student."

"I'm not old enough to get in," Alex pointed out.

"Grace said that if the vet finds out she's related to Dad, he'll think she's not well bred," said Maggie.

"Grace *isn't* well bred; she's Dad's sister," Alex said.

Grace had been living with them ever since their mother had abandoned the family for a warmer climate and her insurance-adjusting boyfriend. Grace was supposed to be helping out, but she wasn't one to do housework. In fact, she was messy and disorganized and nearly doubled Alex's workload of chores. She was always available for conversation, however, and spent much of her free time trying to draw Alex and the twins into highly personal discussions about how they *really* felt about their hair and skin tone, which she then turned into opportunities to test out new cosmetics and innovations in hairdressing.

Grace was around the house quite a lot when she wasn't seeing anyone, but rarely glimpsed when she had a boyfriend. Her relationships never lasted longer than a month. Alex's theory was that her relationships never made it past her first home-cooked meal. Grace was a good, if overly adventurous, hairstylist but an extremely bad cook. Her cooking tended to taste like her hairdressing smelled.

It was just like Grace to expect him to get his father out of the beer tent so she could seduce some innocent vet student. Alex muttered a mild swear word under his breath.

"Don't worry," Maggie assured him. "We'll wait for you outside. You have any problems, just yell."

His sisters behaved as though they were Bruce Lee reincarnated as Caucasian female twins. Their supreme confidence in their physical strength was a source of mystery to Alex, who constantly suspected his body of betrayal on a hundred fronts.

Alex pulled his cowboy hat more firmly down on his head as he followed his sisters away from the dressage rings, past the looming red indoor arena, and over to the large white tent that housed the beer garden.

At the beer garden he stopped to let his sense of dread subside.

Alex glanced from his sisters to the two women who sat behind a table, guarding the entrance to the beer garden. He could hear Kenny Rogers on the sound system inside.

"Hey, honey," said one of the women. She wore a brilliant pink T-shirt with the words SAVE A HORSE, RIDE A COWBOY written on the front.

"You plannin' on joining the party?" she asked.

"Maybe in three years' time he will be," said her fellow door watcher, who had a wandering eye.

"I have to get my dad," he said, trying to focus on the woman's good eye.

"I'm sorry, hon. No minors," said the pink T-shirt lady.

May leaned forward and whispered, "You may have to put the moves on her before they'll let you in."

"It's for the good of the family," Maggie added encouragingly.

Alex ignored his sisters.

The door watchers finally relented. "Okay. But just you. The girls will have to stay out here. We can't have a bunch of kids running in and out of a licensed establishment."

Alex shot his sisters a glance and then walked quickly through the doorway. It took him only a second to spot his dad, who sat near the entrance, deep in conversation with a red-haired woman. His aunt sat across the room beside a man wearing rubber boots and denim coveralls. Grace jerked her head toward Alex's father and grimaced.

Mr. Ford, whose drinking had become heavy and

constant after his wife left, was beginning to sag, as if about to pass out. It was one thing for him to pass out in the lawn chair outside his RV at home, another thing for him to do it in a public beer garden.

Alex walked over and said, as quietly as possible, "Dad?"

Mr. Ford turned his head. "Alex?" he said, as though speaking long distance over the phone to someone he never expected to hear from again.

"Yeah, uh, Maggie and May need to get home. And I'm done for the day. Meredith's going to trailer Turnip home later. So I was thinking maybe we could go."

His father blinked at him and for the millionth time Alex wondered how his father could be so blind drunk yet appear sober to the untrained eye. Handsome, even.

"Are you ready to go?" Alex asked again.

"I can give you a ride later, Brian," said the red-headed lady who sat next to his dad.

Alex frowned at the woman. She had thinning hair that was dyed bright red and eyebrows that had been plucked into surprised arches and penciled in for emphasis. She was dressed in an electric-blue business suit. Alex thought he'd seen her face somewhere before, but couldn't remember where.

"You're old enough to drive yourself, aren't you?" she said, giving Alex a thin smile.

He nodded reluctantly. *Why was she making this more difficult?* Her hot date was about to collapse onto the floor. If that happened it would take at least three people to get him up.

"Thanks," said Alex. "It's just that he's got this thing he has to do."

It was amazing to Alex how many women, with the exception of his mother, seemed to find his father attractive. Especially women of a certain age. Maybe they thought that his used RV dealership made him a good catch. What they didn't know was that his ex-wife had taken a good chunk of his income and his business had begun to falter.

Suddenly Mr. Ford sat upright and shook his head.

"Colette, Ms. Reed. I'd like you to meet my son. He's a fine horseman," he said. "A cowboy."

The red-haired lady gave Alex another insincere smile and he grimly gave one back.

"Okay, Dad. So are you ready?" Alex went to help his father up but was stopped when the woman put a hand on his arm.

"I live just down the road from you."

Alex nodded, not really listening. He wished she'd take her hand off his arm. Once his father was standing he was relatively easy to maneuver. Getting him up was a trick.

"You know, *I* have a horse that needs riding," the lady continued, her hand still on Alex's arm. "I simply don't have the time anymore. Of course, he's a dressage horse and you ride Western so you probably wouldn't be interested."

Now she had his attention.

"He's a very nice boy. A Dutch Warmblood."

Alex kept his face impassive.

"One of these days you and your father should come and see my horse," she said, batting her short, spiky eyelashes at Mr. Ford, who didn't notice.

"Sure, okay. Thanks," said Alex. He gave his father a nudge and was happy to see him rise unsteadily to his feet.

"I'm on Willowbank Road. Not five minutes from your place," continued Ms. Reed. Alex looked at her more closely. She did look familiar. He realized that he'd seen her face on half of the COMING SOON signs around Cedar. She was a realtor who specialized in selling vinyl-sided tract housing built on filled-in wetlands and negotiating deals with private landowners that enabled developers to clear-cut the last remaining pockets of forest around Nanaimo, making room for mini-malls. She finally took her hand off his arm and spoke again to Mr. Ford.

"Good-bye, Brian."

Alex's stomach dropped as his father abruptly swooped down to kiss Ms. Reed's hand. He gave an involuntary sigh of relief when his father completed the move without collapsing on her.

"I will see *you* later," said Mr. Ford to Ms. Reed, throwing her what was probably supposed to be a charming wink but looked more like a gnat had flown into his eye.

Colette Reed smiled coyly.

"This way, Dad," Alex said, propelling his father toward the exit. As he passed by, he glanced at his aunt, who gave him a thumbs-up.

2

Cleo O'Shea

I NEVER SHOULD have let my mom make me switch from plastic horses to real ones. I started collecting model horses when I was a little kid. By the time I turned twelve I had over two hundred of them: bays, chestnuts, palominos, grays, blacks, duns, Thoroughbreds, Appaloosas, Arabs, Morgans, paints, and quarter horses. I had mares, stallions, foals, and yearlings. In my fantasy, I was a veterinarian who'd rescued the horses from abusive owners and nursed them back to health.

My dad, who is a movie producer and director, had the props people from the studio build all these accessories for my horses. I had fences, stables, a racetrack, even miniature trees.

One day my mother met someone at her tennis club, a lady who sent her daughters for riding lessons at a stable out in Lakeview Terrace. The lady, who just happened to be the wife of a studio head, told my mother that the lessons were "wildly expensive." That was all my mom needed to hear. A day later I was booked at the same barn for twice-a-week lessons. One would assume that since I loved plastic horses, I'd have been completely thrilled at the thought of riding real ones. But I wasn't what you'd call an athletic person. Our house had a pool, two housekeepers, and a TV in almost every room. I had my own plastic horse sanctuary. Who'd want to leave?

The day before my first lesson at Performance Ponies Stables, I heard my mom on the phone with the owner.

"I understand that yours is the best school in this area for young *equestriennes*." My mother really drew out that last word and put a heavy French spin on it. "You've come *highly recommended*. Cleo is horse crazy. Simply *mad* about horses. I'm sure you're accustomed to that."

There was a pause.

"Experience? Cleo has read a *lot* of books. She even *collects* horses."

Another pause.

"No, not real horses. Plastic ones. That's right. So, no, I wouldn't say she was a *total* beginner."

Another pause.

"Been around actual horses? Well, no. I don't think so. But she's *always* reading that book about the racehorse. Consuela says she's read it at least a dozen times."

Pause.

"*Actually ridden?* Well, no. Not that I'm aware of."

My mother covered the receiver with her hand and whispered, "Have you ever ridden? At school or anything?"

I shook my head. I'd never been on a horse before. I'd never even been on the same *block* as an actual horse. I was not an agricultural person.

"I'm quite confident she'll have no problems. She comes from a long line of *naturally gifted athletes*."

I had to leave the room. My mother is convinced that weighing only slightly more than a poor quality T-shirt and belonging to a tennis club makes her a two-sport Olympian. She's *delusional* on the point. But that's my mother for you.

When we arrived at the barn for my first lesson, I got out of the car and looked around. The driveway was paved with little red bricks and the barn reminded me of the houses we'd seen when we went on our school trip to Germany. The matching house was dark brown with white trim. It didn't look very California at all.

Chad rolled down the driver's side window.

"You want me to wait for you, C.?"

Chad worked for the car company my parents used. He had genuine sun streaks in his adorably messy surfer hair and crinkly blue eyes. The back of his head was so devastatingly handsome I could barely answer him when he spoke to me. If I'd been smart, I would have kept it that way. It was my increasing ability to say things to Chad that actually landed me in the position I'm in now. But that day I was all about not letting Chad think I was timid, even though there are mice who are much braver than me.

"No thanks," I told him.

"Okay, hon. I'll pick you up in two hours."

My knees buckled a bit at the word *hon*. I must have had a strange expression when I watched the black Lincoln pull away because when I looked up I found a woman watching me with an amused look on her face. She was thin and elongated—like God had meant her to be five feet tall but she somehow got stretched an extra foot—and she had small, bright green eyes and wore no makeup. She had no-nonsense written all over her. She wore rubber boots.

"You're on your own?" the woman asked.

I nodded. My parents had left that morning. They'd be gone for at least three months.

The woman didn't seem concerned. "I'm Dawn," she'd said. "Welcome to the wonderful world of horses."

Dawn taught her students basic equitation, as well as show jumping, hunter-jumper, and dressage. Most of the girls chose to focus on some form of jumping as soon as they finished the basic equitation classes. Not me. I cried all the way through my first two jumping lessons, which involved riding one of the most docile school ponies over trot poles. After that, Dawn decided it would be best if I focused on dressage. That was fine with me. I liked the pre-dictability of dressage and was pretty good at it, at least when I rode Dawn's ponies.

I rode with Dawn for four years. I rode with her until I made the mistake that got me sent here, to Stoneleigh Girls' Equestrian Academy a few weeks ago.

Rather than dealing with me by sending me to military school or therapy, like *normal* parents, my mother and father sentenced me to a riding academy in Canada.

My mom heard about Stoneleigh from some director friend of my father's. The school is one of the only private, girls-only riding academies in North America, located on Vancouver Island, which is 286 miles long and around 50 miles wide, according to the Stoneleigh brochure. There is a city called Victoria at one end, and a bunch of small and medium-sized towns that run down the length of the island. Stoneleigh has low academic standards *and* extremely high tuition—a perfect match for my educational needs! My mother seems convinced that since Canada is so far north I won't be able to get into any trouble here. She seems to have confused it with Switzerland or something. My parents didn't tour Stoneleigh before they enrolled me or they might have realized that they aren't getting what they're paying for.

My parents bought me my own horse right before they shipped me off to Stoneleigh Girls' Equestrian Academy, conveniently located here in Nowhereville, British Columbia, Canada. My new horse, Tandava, is a seventeen-hand Holsteiner mare. Holsteiners are this breed of German sport horses bred to be very good at jumping and dressage. She's a warmblood, but her temperament leans more to the hot-blooded side of things. Some might even say the completely crazy side.

On the sales video my mom got, Tandy was described as an "extravagant mover with international potential." She's also what people sometimes refer to as *a lot of horse*, which is the polite way to say better handled by a professional and definitely too much horse for a sixteen-year-old who's only been riding for four years. Today I am supposed to ride a third-level test, my first in competition. The third-level test is my lousy coach's idea. And it would be a fine idea except for the fact that I am a first-level dressage rider. On my good days. And I haven't had a good day since I got here to Stoneleigh Academy, not quite a month ago. Add to that the fact that I'm scared of my new horse and you can see why I wasn't in any big rush to get going.

"Hello? Hello? Earth to Cleo?"

Phillipa's voice penetrated my thoughts like a drill bit.

"Sorry?" I said, looking up from the blank page in my Journal of Despair (J.O.D.) that I'd been staring at for at least five minutes.

"Aren't you going to get ready? You're on in like forty minutes. You haven't even tacked up."

.Phillipa and I sat in the school's royal-blue camp chairs with the Stoneleigh Academy logo printed on the back at the end of a row of stalls. We might not be the best riders at the Fall Fling Horse Show at Beban Park, but we definitely had the nicest folding chairs. As soon as we sat down, Phillipa started giving me a running commentary on everyone who rode past. I'd been pretending to make notes in my J.O.D. and fantasizing about being somewhere else. Anywhere else, actually.

"Cleo? Are you listening to me?"

Relentless. The girl was relentless. I was hoping to just sort of miss the class, pretend I forgot my time or something. But Phillipa, with her constant thoughtful reminders, was making that impossible.

This was my first show on Vancouver Island and so far it reminded me of every other show I'd been to, except that the arena and rings and barns and stuff were a bit more downscale and the people weren't quite as tan. Or thin. Other than that it was the same basic scene: tidy girls in shiny boots bitching out their parents, people fussing around with their horses, dust, and hot dogs.

The main difference is that here I felt like an outsider. Not only because I just moved here, but because I go to Stoneleigh, which seems sort of isolated from the rest of the riding community. Even Phillipa is treated like a Stoneleigh interloper, and she grew up on the island.

Phillipa is the only other dressage rider at my new school, and so far, she's my only friend. She's been attending Stoneleigh since she was in Grade Five and I think I may be her only friend, too, which is verging on tragic. We started hanging out as soon as I got here.

"I can't believe Svetlana didn't even come," Phillipa groaned. "She is the worst coach ever."

I couldn't disagree with her. Phil says there are lots of good coaches in the area, but they refuse to teach at Stoneleigh because Phil and I are the only ones who take dressage lessons regularly. Half the time coaches arrive to find that dressage lessons have been canceled for a jumping event or they have to try and teach in a ring filled with jumps and poles. It probably doesn't help that Stoneleigh's only two dressage students aren't very good.

Phillipa has a decent seat and hands, but she's kind of passive. It's obvious that she'd rather be braiding her horse's mane than riding him. If her horse, Hernando, wasn't so good-natured she'd be in real trouble because she's the opposite of a disciplinarian.

"Have you seen my mom?" asked Phillipa. "She said she'd be here by now. She's bringing me my boots."

That was enough to get me out of my chair. Phil's mother is competitive enough for both of them. She's as skinny and hard as Phil is plump and gentle. She comes to school every weekend to watch Phil ride and she spends half her time lobbing underhanded insults at the competition (me) and the rest of her time gossiping. It's enough to make me appreciate my own absentee parents.

From what I can tell, Phil's parents aren't that well-off and they've had to make lots of sacrifices to send her to Stoneleigh. As much as I want to be supportive of the working class and everything, they are totally wasting their money. Phillipa isn't ever going to the Olympics and Stoneleigh may be expensive, but that doesn't mean it provides some superb education or anything. It's not like my old school, Marlborough, which was all about academics. As far as I can tell, the majority of the girls at Stoneleigh are okay students and very serious riders. Then there are the screwed-up rich girls who just happen to be somewhat into horses. They've been sent to Stoneleigh in an attempt to keep them on their horses and out of jail. It doesn't take a genius to figure out which category I fit into. But at least I fit in somewhere. That's more than poor old Phil can say.

As I walked over to Tandava's stall I wiped at my face. I could feel my hand shaking. Why was I so nervous? I used to love shows, but that's because Dawn was there, handling everything. In California I competed on Dawn's perfectly trained school ponies. I was like Attila the Hun in the ring—you know, I conquered everybody in sight. On Tandava, I'm going to be more like the villagers Attila slaughtered.

All my black thoughts disappeared when I saw Tandava's head poking over the stall door. She nickered a greeting and reached for a treat. Even her head was gorgeous.

"This is the kind of horse that could take you all the way," the voice-over on her sales video had said. Yeah, all the way to Christopher Reeve–ville if I'm not careful.

The day Tandava arrived at Stoneleigh, she bolted as she was backing out of the deluxe air-conditioned trailer that my parents hired to bring her to school. The driver, barn staff, and students spent an hour tracking her before they finally found her in the parking lot of a small liquor store in a mini-mall a few miles away. She was surrounded by nervous shoppers and a couple of those Canadian RCMPs, who didn't seem to know whether they should take out their guns or their lassoes. Poor horse. I sympathized with her. I wanted to run away the first day I got here, too.

Since then she's expressed her feelings about the move by bucking me off a few times, kicking holes in her stall, and biting the horse in the paddock next to her. If my parents hadn't thrown the headmistress a few bucks for the new indoor arena fund, I bet we'd be looking for a new home for her. And for me.

According to Phil, Stoneleigh girls have a reputation for having too much money and not enough supervision. The locals don't seem to find that a winning combination. They don't want their kids getting mixed up with us. You'd think that with Phil and me being dressage riders and not jumpers, people might cut us some slack, but so far no one was breaking any legs coming over to say hello.

I caught some other girls around my age giving Tandava an intimidated look when I took off her sheet. She's a spectacular-looking horse, but if anyone around here had seen me ride her before they wouldn't look so concerned.

After running a cloth over her to remove every last speck of dust, I looked down at myself. I was a disaster. As usual. There was a big black smudge on my white breeches, the kind that would just get worse if I tried to rub it off.

I could feel sweat soaking all the way through my white blouse and black jacket. My nerves were getting worse by the second and Tandava could sense it. By the time I had the saddle on she was pawing at the ground and shifting nervously around.

I got the bridle on, with difficulty, and led her over to a mounting block, but she refused to stand still and nearly dragged me off it several times before some woman took pity and came over and held her while I got on.

All around me girls were being given a leg up by Mommy or Coach, while Daddy held the horse. I tried not to notice people looking at me as I rode over to the warm-up ring. Tandava barely touched the ground. It was like trying to ride a blob of mercury or a vial of nitroglycerine. She kept flinging her head around and overbending her neck. *Sit up straight*, I told myself sternly. *At least pretend you've got the situation under control.*

The fairgrounds were packed with people and horses and the afternoon went from freezing to scorching every time the sun came out from behind the gray clouds.

In the warm-up ring Tandava spooked at everything, including fallen leaves and stray dust particles. People were really staring now. She kept backing up instead of moving forward, jogging when she was supposed to be walking, and cantering on the spot. I'd only been riding for a couple of minutes and already Tandy was dripping with sweat. Her neck was lathered with white foam where the reins touched her but her mouth was totally dry. I felt my own sweat trickling into my boots.

Every time Tandava sensed danger, which was approximately every 0.4 seconds or so, she leaped into the air. I tried to hang on and kept muttering "sorry, sorry" to all the riders whose horses spooked as we went bolting past.

I gave up trying to tire her out before it was our turn to ride. I could have run her all day and it wouldn't have made a difference. I jumped off and led her out of the warm-up ring. Her mahogany sides heaved and her flanks were black with sweat. Her nostrils flared, showing scarlet in their depths.

I took a moment to squeeze the sweat out of my gloves, praying that I'd survive the next half hour. When I finished, I noticed someone watching us. It was a boy. Not just any boy. A *cowboy*. I straightened and tried to pretend I was just taking it easy before it was my turn to ride, very much like a genuine cowboy would before getting on his roping horse or bucking bronco or whatever.

The boy, who had very dark eyes and was wearing sexy cowboy gear—a big silver belt buckle, shiny, pointy-toed cowboy boots, and a huge light-gray cowboy hat—gave me a little lip curl. If fact, I think what he gave me was a cool, genuine cowboy smile. If I wasn't about to be killed, I totally would have smiled back.

"Number forty-eight! Number forty-eight! You're up next," called out the lady with the clipboard, looking for the next victim.

"Oh God, that's me," I muttered. Before I went, I looked again at the cowboy and he nodded. I couldn't stand the thought of him watching my humiliation, so I led Tandy to a mounting block a bit farther away.

Four minutes later I tried to trot Tandava around the outside of the ring while I waited for the bell to ring to signal that we could enter, but she insisted on cantering. It was like riding a guided missile without the guidance part.

Dressage is all about harmony between horse and rider—calmness, suppleness, submission, plus not getting killed. All I had to do was pretend like I had things under control.

The bell tinkled and the whipper-in pulled back the piece of fence at *A* so we could enter. Dressage rings have letters around the perimeter to show you where you're supposed to go. We entered at *A* at what was supposed to be a collected trot but was actually a very slow canter. I practically had to wrestle Tandy to get her to stop in the middle of the ring at *X*. When she did finally stop it was at an unknown letter off to the side of *X*. Let's call it *Q*.

I saluted the judge, not daring to look at him. Tandava surged beneath me, ready to explode. I had to get moving again.

We tracked left at *C* and proceeded in a collected trot. Or in some weird variation of passage. I'm not sure which. It wasn't my idea.

From *S* to *V* we were supposed to do a shoulder-in. This turned into a half pass across the diagonal, which landed us in no-man's-land on the other side of the ring. *How was I supposed to get back to where we were supposed to be? What were we supposed to be doing?* Back when I rode Dawn's schoolmaster ponies it took about fifteen minutes to get from one end of the ring to the other. On Tandava it took about six strides.

I turned Tandy in a small circle and the bell rang, signaling that I was off course. Frankly, I was just glad to be alive, but there was much more to come.

L to S, half pass left. Tandava was really gathering speed now. It was like trying to half halt a steam engine.

M, X, K, change rein at medium trot. Tandava streaked off at just under the speed of light. I only barely brought her back so we could make the corner. My head was sweating so much that my hat slipped sideways over one eye. I was riding blind!

K, collected trot. Yeah, right.

F, X, H, change rein, extended trot. With a bit of

canter thrown in toward the end.

R to P, shoulder-in right. Also known as rush sideways with head thrust in the air.

Okay, okay. I took a deep breath. The test slowed down a bit now. I was going to get through this. Tandava's huffing and puffing made her sound more like an angry rhino than a horse.

Between P and L, half circle right ten meters. Or fifteen if your steering fails. ·

L to R, half pass right. Then left. Then right again.

C, halt. (Praise *God!*) *Reinback four steps.* Or refuse to budge. Whatever works.

Proceed at medium walk. Or at slow, disobedient jog.

Between G and H, shorten stride, half turn on haunches right. Or have horse rear onto hind legs, causing rider to emit small scream of fear.

Walk around a bit more, unsure where to go. Hear off-course bell again. Force self not to finger person ringing it.

Aha! Suddenly remember to break into collected canter on left lead at *A.* Or break into right lead to show that your aids—hand and leg signals—are 100 percent ineffective.

A to C, three loop serpentine-simple change of lead

each time crossing centerline. Or zigzag crazily around ring at canter with short breaks for fits of bucking.

H to K, medium canter. The less said about this, the better.

K, collected canter. Or continue with increasingly out of control extended canter, as horse wishes.

P, circle left. Use radical lean similar to that seen in barrel-racing ponies.

P to S, change rein with flying change between centerline and S. Give two violent bucks at centerline and bolt toward *S*. Run right over railing, knocking down half the ring. Go flying into the crowd, scattering kids and horses and dogs and spectators. Hang on for dear life as horse makes for the soccer field at warp speed while off-course bell rings madly behind you.

Be grateful that you didn't run over cute cowboy on the way out of the ring. He probably walked away in disgust at your incredibly foul performance.

Cleo

AFTER I BARELY survived what was probably the worst third-level test ever ridden at any Fall Fling in history, I put my foot down. "I want to come home. I've learned my lesson," I said.

"Honey, you can't come home. We are in Africa on the shoot until at least December. And you've proven that you can't be trusted on your own. You have poor judgment."

"That's ridiculous," I said. "What happened with Chad was almost like an accident. I was defrauded! Like an elderly person."

"*You* were defrauded!" exclaimed my mother. "*We* were the ones who were defrauded! By you!"

"That's not fair," I said, even though she was basically right.

"As I said, you've proven you can't be left alone. You are staying at school and that's final."

"But I don't want to stay here! Tandava nearly killed me. The coach here is a nightmare. I have a *sprained ankle*! From *falling off*!" My voice was starting to climb.

I took a deep breath to center myself.

"So you want me dead. That's it, isn't it?"

"Cleo, we've found you a fabulous situation there. You're in *Canada*. At a girls' *equestrienne* school."

"It's a school for people who *jump* their horses. They don't even *teach* dressage here."

"So jump, darling."

"I don't want to jump. I'm not into jumping! I goddamn *hate* jumping. Don't you ever listen?" I shrieked.

I saw Phillipa's eyes grow big. Apparently she doesn't curse at her parents.

"Calm down, Cleo. Being negative is never a positive option," said my mother. Then, without warning, her voice dropped two registers and she snarled, "Tell him that is out of the question. We are not going to be blackmailed into meeting that has-been's every demand. He wants to leave, fine. He can *walk* back to the U.S."

"Mom?"

"Sorry, honey, I am just talking to David's agent."

"God!" I shouted. "You're not listening to me."

"Don't be silly."

"Is Daddy there? Does he want to talk to me?"

"Honey, you know he's on set and can't be disturbed over minor things."

"Nearly getting killed is not a minor thing! I can't stay here. The school sucks. The people suck. And my riding's just getting worse."

I quickly looked over at Phillipa. She was staring at the floor.

"Tell you what," said my mother. "We'll get you a new instructor. We'll even get you a new horse if that's what it takes."

"Whatever," I said. "Do what you want. I'll just be over here doing street drugs to deal with the pain of my broken ankle."

"Oh, Cleo," said my mother. "Please don't take anything that isn't prescribed by a doctor. Darling, I have to go. Daddy says hello." Without missing a beat her voice switched back into bitch mode. "That is not going to happen. You tell that lazy bastard that he better get his ass back on set *right now* or I'll get him blacklisted with every director in Hollywood *and* Africa. You hear me?" Then she hung up.

I slammed the phone down on the desk a couple of times, then put the receiver back in the stand.

"The phone still works," I said, picking it up and turning it on so Phillipa could hear the dial tone.

"Good," she said.

"And, uh, you don't really suck. I just said that."

Phillipa's round pink face flushed slightly. She hesitated for a moment and then asked, "*Are* you doing drugs?"

"Just Tylenol."

"And what was that about getting defrauded?"

"Oh, that. There was just this thing with this guy back home. It's nothing."

"Okay," she said. "Well, I guess I should head back to my room."

"Seriously. I'm not on drugs. I'm just high-strung," I said.

"If you say so," said Phillipa, but she smiled when she said it.

She really is a nice girl. Someday I may tell her about the little incident with Chad. Actually, since I've brought it up here, I might as well get the whole thing off my chest. I never should have gotten in the front seat. That's where the trouble started.

Chad drove me to riding lessons for almost four years. I looked forward to those drives out to the barn for my dressage lessons. We had these terrific conversations, although I didn't say much. I didn't need to. Chad was extremely charming and open. He was twenty-two and he talked to me like I was an adult instead of a teenager. He said I was easy to talk to, that none of the other people he drove listened as well as I did. He said I listened like a much older girl.

For the first three years and seven months, I rode in the back of the car. Then one day I came running out to the car with my sneakers untied, carrying my boot bag. I was late and Dawn was going to be pissed. Chad had been waiting for at least fifteen minutes. I tried never to be late for my drives with Chad. They were half the reason I loved riding lessons so much.

"I'm so sorry," I said as I ran to the driver's window, which he had rolled down.

"No prob, C." He hesitated and then looked deep into my eyes. "Why don't you hop in up front here?"

I felt my heart flutter.

"Okay. Sure."

"It's easier for us to talk that way," he said as he

grinned at me. "I want to know what's happening in the Kingdom of Cleopatra."

I looked back at the house. No one was watching. My parents were in Germany, and they never looked out the window even when they were home.

"Hang on," said Chad, getting out of the car.

He followed me around to the passenger side. His suntanned hand brushed my arm as he took my boot bag. "Let me get that," he said, as he put it in the backseat. Then he opened the passenger door for me.

"My lady," he said as he gestured for me to get in.

With him opening my door and everything, it suddenly felt like I was on a date. A real date, my first. And it was with the most beautiful guy in the world.

That was the last time I got into the front seat in our driveway. After that I got into the backseat, as usual, but once we were out of sight of the house he pulled over and I got into the front seat so I could hear him better.

One day, after I'd been sitting up beside him for a few weeks, he asked if I wanted to play a little game.

"Sure. Yeah!" I said. If he'd suggested we play a quick round of Russian Roulette, I'd have been right there.

"It's like truth or dare. Only there's no dare part."

"Okay," I said, already feeling us getting closer. More intimate.

"It's kind of a sexy little game," he said. "I think you're going to like it."

"Okay," I said, trying not to sound as breathless as I felt.

He went first. He told me that he liked my eyes.

I told him that I thought he was a really excellent driver.

"Thanks, hon," he said, which made my thighs go all quivery.

"You look really good in those riding pants," he said.

I made a noise between a squeak and a giggle.

"I love your hair." I didn't mention that for almost four years I'd been in love with the back of his head.

"Thanks, babe," he said.

Oh, I loved the sexy little game, which is how I always thought of it. We played it every time he drove me to and from the barn. He told me that he dreamed of becoming a competitive surfer. He told me how hard it was to find surfing sponsors. How his employers at the car service company weren't cool about giving him time off to compete.

Because of my sheltered existence and my school's annoying emphasis on academics and athletics as opposed to sophisticated life experience, I only had so many secrets to share. When your whole life consists of going to school, watching TV, and taking riding lessons, you tend not to build up much of a store of secrets. I could have told him that I felt lonely most of the time, except when he was driving me to lessons, but then it would have been a depressing little game instead of a sexy one.

We even shared very small secrets. Household secrets. I used a Sonicare toothbrush. He used Crest Whitestrips. He told me where he kept the spare key to his apartment. I told him where we kept ours. It was all part of the sexy little game!

"I really feel like I can tell you anything," he said, one day after we'd been playing the game for a few months.

I tried to control my face. I felt like he just told me he loved me.

"Look, I'll prove it. Here's the PIN number for my bank card," he said.

I was so moved I told him the security code for our house alarm.

He turned the car into a strange neighborhood and pulled over.

"You're amazing, C.," he said. "I love that we have no secrets."

Then he leaned over and kissed me. He slipped his hand between my knees. He tasted like salt and mint breath spray. After we kissed, he drove me the rest of the way home with his hand on my thigh, like I was his girlfriend. Or his wife. We stayed like that until he pulled over a couple of blocks from our place so I could get into the backseat.

I left the next morning for a four-day riding camp. My parents were in Budapest. When I got back I discovered our house crawling with cops. They'd been called by Consuela, our housekeeper, who arrived after her day off to discover the house had been robbed. Stripped bare. I instantly knew that Chad was responsible because whoever robbed us hadn't broken any locks or set off the alarm system. I was sad that his dream of becoming a pro surfer and traveling to all the big competitions required that he take not only all our antique vases, but also our art, furniture, electronics, and carpets. Still, he'd left my plastic horse collection, which I took as evidence that he loved me, even if he had gone a little overboard with stealing the rest of our stuff.

The cops and my parents were extremely suspicious, but I tried to throw them off the scent. I wasn't about to rat out the man I loved and who probably loved me. My parents, especially my dad, were furious that they'd had to leave in the middle of the shoot. I didn't bow to pressure.

"No," I told them. "I don't have any idea how anyone could have discovered the code."

I waited a few days until things had calmed down before I went to see Chad. I wanted to wish him well in his surfing and let him know that even though our house was basically an empty shell, his love for me was keeping me warm and comfortable and I was willing to wait for him to achieve all his surfing goals before we got married.

I didn't know where Chad lived but he'd told me where he liked to surf, so I caught a bus to Manhattan Beach. It turned out that Manhattan Beach went on for what felt like approximately a hundred miles. I was on the verge of giving up when I finally spotted Chad. He was sitting on the sand, his surfboard beside him. As soon as I saw him, I knew

I'd done the right thing. *Look at him,* I thought. *He's financially secure for the first time in his life, thanks to me.* I walked quickly toward him.

"Chad!" I cried. "Chad!"

He turned at the sound of my voice. When I was about twenty feet away I broke into a run.

"Chad!" I said.

He kind of jumped to his feet and held out his arms. I went to throw myself into them. Only it turns out he wasn't holding his arms out in a romantic, catch-a-flying-girl kind of way. He was holding them out in a *defensive* way, so I kind of bounced off him.

He looked around. "Cleo," he said without much enthusiasm.

"Chad," I said.

"Dude, what are you doing here?"

Dude?

"But I just wanted—"

"Cleo, man. You shouldn't be here."

Man?

"But you . . . we. What about us?"

I looked and finally noticed the tall, thin woman he'd been sitting beside. If I had to describe her in a police lineup, I'd have used the word *model-y*.

He patted the air, indicating that I should pipe down.

"Chad?" said the undeniably hot girl, who still hadn't gotten to her feet. It was a good thing, too, because she was nearly as tall as me when she was sitting.

"Dude, you have to split," said Chad. "This isn't cool."

"Chad? What's going on?" asked the girl. When the girl squinted she looked just like Kate Moss.

"It's cool. This is Cleo. I work for her parents. She's just a—"

That's when the big guy in the surfer shorts walked up.

"Fancy meeting you two here," he said. Then he dug around in his shorts and pulled out a private investigator's I.D.

"Chad?" said Kate Moss.

"Chad?" I said, still trying to figure out what was happening.

"Look, man, I barely know this girl. She's been coming on to me. . . . It's like she's obsessed or something."

"Chad?" said Kate Moss again.

"You took our TVs," I said.

Chad spoke to the investigator like I wasn't even there.

"It was her idea," he said. "She asked me to steal their stuff."

"Chad," said the investigator in a disappointed voice.

The point of this story is that I have occasionally displayed what my mother refers to as "faulty decision-making." But I am completely confident that my worst decisions are behind me. I'm pretty certain, anyhow.

Three days after I told my mom I wanted to leave Stoneleigh, I was pulled out of class for a phone call. Right away I was convinced that my parents had been killed by one of those giant parasites they have everywhere in Africa. You know, those ten-foot worms that burrow their way into the skin of your foot and have to be pulled out of your elbow. Maybe they stepped outside and were run down by a herd of stampeding rhinos or mauled by a pack of wild jackals. I wish my parents could occasionally work on movies set somewhere normal, but it's always the Arctic Circle or Timbuktu or some place.

I walked into the office, and the secretary pointed

me toward the office of Ms. Green, the headmistress.

Ms. Green's face was a mottled, reddish color and her forehead was furrowed as though she was busy trying to work out very complicated math. I recognized the look. It meant she'd been talking to my mother. At least my mother was still alive.

"Here's Cleo now," said Ms. Green, and quickly handed me the phone.

"Hello?"

"Honey! Good news!"

I flicked a glance at Ms. Green.

"Uh, hi, Mom. Why are you calling me here? This is the principal's office."

"I'm in Africa, darling," she said, as though that explained everything. "I just wanted to let you know that we've found you a new instructor. Instructors, actually. I've arranged everything with Ms. Green. Your horse will be moved to the new barn and until we get you a car, a staff member from the school will drive you to and fro. A *female* staff member. A Mrs. Dirt, I believe."

"You mean Mrs. Mudd. How did—?"

"We were *incredibly* lucky to get Fergus and Ivan. It took considerable coaxing from my contacts to get them to take you on."

"Who—?"

"They were trainers in *Europe*," she said, her voice going all breathy. "I got their names from Princess Fontania. She's *European royalty*. Minor royalty, but still. She's fabulously wealthy and marvelously eccentric. She lives here in the hotel with the man who used to be her footman. It would be absolutely scandalous if the two of them weren't at least eighty-five years old. She used to ride dressage and she swears Fergus and Ivan are the best. Can you believe that they retired to Vancouver Island recently, not far at all from your school? Okay, darling, must fly. One of the caterers just made eye contact with our lead actress and she won't come out of her trailer."

The phone went dead and I handed the receiver to Ms. Green, who raised one eyebrow as she hung it up.

My new coaches didn't seem very thrilled to meet me, or Phillipa, whom I brought along for moral support.

When we got out of the Stoneleigh truck, the tall, elegant one, who had a thick head of white hair, crossed his arms over his chest, and said, "One, we only agreed to take one. This is two." He spoke to the shorter, bald man beside him as though Phil and I weren't standing right in front of them.

Mrs. Mudd, the school driver, smirked.

"I just drive 'em," she said.

The short bald one, who had clear blue eyes that crinkled at the corners, held out his hand to Phillipa. "Hello, love," he said.

Phillipa blushed madly. "Oh, no. She's Cleo," she giggled. "I'm just her friend."

"There is nothing more important than a friend, my dear. It's a pleasure to make your acquaintance."

Phil's face was so red it looked like her head was going to explode. She stared, awestruck, at her hand as though it had turned to gold.

Then the short man turned to me. "And hello to you, my dear. We've heard so much about you."

That made it my turn to blush. He was very courtly. I could totally picture him knowing a princess.

"I'm Fergus and this is Ivan," the short man continued, nodding toward the tall one, who stood behind him. "We understand you're interested in joining us for dressage lessons."

The tall one sniffed rudely. He wore a white blouse with poufy sleeves and tall, shiny brown boots over breeches. He looked like an old, bitchy pirate. Minus the earring.

"You want me to unload the horse now?" asked Mrs. Mudd.

Fergus, who was working the English country-gentleman look of brown cords and soft green quilted vest over a cabled Irish knit sweater, blinked quickly. "You mean you've brought the horse here? We haven't even discussed Cleo's needs."

"I'm not pulling that horse trailer around for my health," said Mrs. Mudd. "Anyway, I don't care about the details. I just drive these little girls and their ponies where I'm told. And I was told that this particular girl was moving her horse here. And good riddance, too, because that mare is a pain in the ass to load, if you catch my drift."

The tall, white-haired, blouse-wearing man leveled an offended glare at Mrs. Mudd, who didn't seem disturbed by it.

"Well," said Fergus, looking from Phil to me. "Isn't this fun?"

Mrs. Mudd didn't waste any more time with idle chitchat. She stalked around to the back of the six-horse trailer and unloaded Tandava, who came out at her usual backward gallop. Mrs. Mudd handed me the lead rope. As soon as I took it, she climbed into the truck to read her novel.

Tandy turned around and around in anxious circles as I tried to hang on to her. "This is Tandava," I said.

"She's Cleo's horse," added Phil.

"You don't say," said Fergus.

Ivan just stared. Finally, he pointed. At me or at Tandy. I couldn't tell which, so I just stood there while she stepped all over herself as she snorted and looked wildly around.

"Phillipa, be a love and help Cleo take off the mare's rug and shipping boots," said Fergus.

Cautiously, Phil and I got Tandy's gear off.

Ivan stared at her some more, his face working with disapproval. Then he tossed his head and waved his hand. If we'd been on board a pirate ship I'd have thought he was giving the signal to push somebody overboard. Luckily Fergus was there to interpret.

"Sweetheart, Ivan would like you to walk her out so he can see her move."

I walked Tandava past them.

"Trot," instructed Fergus. I quickened my pace until Tandy broke into a trot.

I went as far down the driveway as I could and then slowed her to a walk and led her back.

"My goodness, you have a very nice horse there," said Fergus.

"What a terrible, terrible waste," said Ivan, before he turned on his heel and stalked off toward the house.

We enjoyed another awkward silence until Fergus clapped his hands and rubbed them briskly together. "Not to worry, dear girls. He'll come around. Let's get this beautiful lady settled, shall we?"

Limestone, Ivan and Fergus's farm, is on the edge of a lake. I don't think it's a swimming lake or anything. It's more like the kind of lake that swans and ducks hang out in. A dark forest borders one side of the property and on the other side green fields roll all the way down to the lake. Fergus and Ivan's house is nestled at the base of the hill. The house suits the setting perfectly, with windows on all sides. The stables and indoor arena and outdoor ring are just as attractive as the house. I was actually a little surprised at how nice the whole place was. You have to hand it to my mom. Even from Africa she can locate a money situation.

"This is awesome," I said to Fergus.

"Hmmm, yes," he said. "Slightly underused but awesome, as you so charmingly put it."

We put Tandava in a small paddock near the barn to let her calm down and have a look at her new surroundings, and then Fergus gave us a tour. I could see what he meant by underused. There was an eight-stall barn, an indoor arena, a regulation-size outdoor dressage ring, and fully fenced fields as far as I could see. And hardly any horses.

Fergus led us toward one of them, an older horse with a swayback and a big belly. "This is Honoré. She's a retired broodmare."

Phillipa put out her hand, and Honoré gently sniffed at it.

"She's sweet," said Phil as Honoré snuffled at her hair.

"Honoré is trained to Grand Prix. She's produced five foals, four of which have earned top honors at European sport horse competitions. This gentle lady has earned her retirement," said Fergus.

He led us to the next pasture, where a big bay horse grazed at a distance. Fergus didn't say anything; he just stood there and all of a sudden the horse lifted its head, sniffed, then came tearing toward us at a full gallop. It slid to a halt, and poked its head over the fence. Fergus reached out and gave it a scratch.

"This is Ranier. He's an Oldenburg stallion."

I saw Phillipa's eyes widen as she took in the

horse's height and his massive chest.

"He's huge," she said.

"Ah yes, that he is. He's a lovely horse. Very talented. Ranier was Ivan's last competition horse. He is also trained to Grand Prix, but like his owners and stablemates, he's retired."

Fergus turned and walked down to the field nearest the lake. A white horse was waiting for us when we arrived at the fence.

"And this is Princess. She's an Andalusian/Dutch Warmblood cross."

"Is she trained all the way, too?" Phil asked.

"Nearly," he said. "She has some work to do on her reading comprehension, but other than that she's quite accomplished."

Princess, with her big, soft, black curious eyes, did look just about smart enough to read.

"Are you saying you have *three* Grand Prix–level horses here?" Phil said.

"Two *retired* Grand Prix horses. Princess is a retired Prix St. Georges schoolmaster."

"I thought there were only five horses trained to Grand Prix on the whole island," said Phil.

"You've got this huge place for three retired horses?" I said. "Why?"

"Perhaps you think we should move our retired horses into a nice condominium? We've only recently moved here. Who knows what will come our way? Perhaps there will be more surprises like you two."

Phillipa shook her head. "It's just Cleo. I have to leave my horse at school."

"That's a shame, dear. But think of it this way—eventually Ivan will get over his pique and give Cleo a lesson. Then she'll be sorry she's not still at school with you."

I looked at Phil. That's exactly what I was afraid of.

Alex

ALEX TOLD HIS trainer on the way to the tack store. Afterward he felt naked.

"Come again?" Meredith asked.

"Dressage. I'm thinking of switching to dressage."

"Is this some twisted way of punishing me for going to Texas?"

"No, that's not it. I'm just interested, I guess. I've always been sort of interested."

"And you're just telling me now? We could have done more English. You could have shown hunter under saddle. I just didn't think you were interested." Meredith cast him a sideways glance. "You know, if you switch to dressage your dad's going to freak."

"It has nothing to do with him," Alex said, even

though he knew she was right. But if he was ever going to switch, now was the time. In a few days Meredith was leaving the local barn she managed to take over a big quarter-horse breeding and training operation in Texas.

"Well, they say dressage is the basis for everything," Meredith said, as she pulled the truck into the parking lot. "Maybe I can explain that to your dad. Tell him even the real old-time cowboys use dressage techniques."

Alex stared gratefully after his trainer as he followed her into the tack store.

Lately she'd been asking after his friends at school and he knew she was probably trying to establish that he had some. School, for Alex, was just the place he went between rides. He had exactly two acquaintances there. Chris was a quiet, blond boy who carried a black sketchpad everywhere. He wore sweater vests and old cardigans and had to be asked to remove his headphones if you wanted to say anything to him. Sofia was a round-faced Chinese Canadian girl who hid her sardonic sense of humor behind long silences and her lush good looks behind unfashionable eyeglasses and shapeless T-shirts with dorky logos. The three of them hung around together but they didn't talk much.

When Meredith asked about his friends, Alex told her about how he and Chris and Sofia went out to eat and to movies on the weekends. His stories were total fabrications, but he could tell she liked hearing them. Sometimes lying was the best thing you could do for someone you cared about.

Kind of like how people seemed to appreciate hearing that he had a girlfriend. The girlfriend was a lie, too, but over time she'd become nearly real to him. He used her when other guys were making jokes about sex and girls and he felt like he had to say *something*. He'd never come out and told Chris and Sofia about his imaginary girlfriend directly, but he'd dropped a few big hints, alluding to a "certain someone" he'd met at a horse show out of town and whom he was "pretty into." It probably wasn't necessary since neither of them ever said anything about their own romances. Sofia didn't seem to want anyone to notice that she was a girl, and Chris seemed worried that someone would ask him to turn down his music and have an actual conversation. *The three of us are very strange*, thought Alex, with a certain degree of satisfaction.

"So I guess we should be finding you some dressage gear," said Meredith as she perused the shelves full of supplements and ointments. "I mean, since you're making the big switch."

Alex nodded, even though he had already collected much of what he'd need to begin his dressage training. While some boys hoarded pornography, Alex had a stash of dressage paraphernalia that he'd collected over the years hidden in his sock drawer. Included were the video of the dressage competition in the last Olympics, a pair of tan breeches, and some English riding boots that he'd purchased for half price on a trip out of town, as well as a copy of *The Complete Training of Horse and Rider in the Principles of Classical Horsemanship* by Alois Podhajsky. Today he hadn't planned on buying anything except a new pair of gloves.

"Well, if you're going to start riding dressage you're going to need a lot more than just new gloves." Meredith reached down for a long dressage whip and handed it to Alex. "You're definitely going to need this. Your poor old Turnip's going to have to pick it up a few notches."

Alex inspected the whip and was suddenly gripped by an intense desire to have it. He became aware of another customer, a short bald man with clear blue eyes, who seemed to be smiling to himself.

"Oh, come on. Just buy the damn thing," said Meredith. "It's on sale and it's already the cheapest one in the store. That and your gloves and you're on your way to a major shopping binge. When that's done, you can start saving for dressage lessons. From what I hear, those don't come cheap."

Alex groaned.

He loved the feel of the dressage whip in his hands. He felt like brandishing it around the store, like fencing with it or dancing with it. Alex was reminded of the freedom he used to feel passaging around the living room on his imaginary dressage horse. Between the gloves and the whip and the confession, he was as happy as he'd been in weeks as he walked up to the register.

Moments later his elation was gone as the clerk informed him that his family account was overdue. Badly overdue. Face burning, Alex stared at the counter. It was crowded with horse treats and horse-themed jewelry. He was uncomfortably aware that the bald man he'd seen earlier was behind him in line. In the close confines of the tack shop the man would be able to hear every word the clerk spoke.

"I'm sorry," the clerk said. "Just ask your father to come in and bring your account up to date. We can hold these things for you."

Alex couldn't seem to move, so Meredith gently took his arm and pulled him out of the store.

The two of them got into Meredith's old diesel truck with the STARFLEET ACADEMY and I ♥ QUARTER HORSES bumper stickers in the rear window. They sat in silence for a moment.

Finally Alex spoke. "I guess my dad must've forgot to pay."

Meredith bit her lip. "I don't think so."

"What do you mean?"

"Your dad's a little behind in his bills."

"You mean he hasn't paid you either?"

Meredith shrugged and tucked a stray piece of hair behind her ear.

"Why didn't you tell me?"

"I'm sure he's good for it," she said.

Alex frowned.

"Look, Alex, you have talent. Real talent. Look at how well you've done on Turnip. A good part of the credit goes to you. Doesn't matter what kind of riding you do—English, Western—you've got good hands and a really nice feel for horses. That's a rare thing."

Alex couldn't believe his ears. Meredith wasn't one to throw compliments around.

"Are you serious?" he asked.

"Don't push your luck, or I'll take it back. Now about this money thing," she said. "Horses are expensive. Unless you're a silver-spoon type, you're going to struggle sometimes. But think of it this way: At least you've got talent. A lot of these big-money types, they've got cash all right, but you can't buy a seat and hands like yours."

The knock on the window made both of them jump. Alex turned to see the man who'd been in line behind him and he quickly rolled down his window.

"I couldn't help but hear that you're looking to find instruction in the fine art of dressage."

The man pronounced the word *dressage* in two parts: "dray-sage." With his shiny bald head and clothes in muted and tasteful shades of green and brown, he looked like the sort of person who should have a pair of trained Border collies trotting at his heel as he strode through a field full of sheep.

The man handed a piece of paper through the window.

"Give us a call, ducks. We might be able to help you."

Alex, surprised, took the piece of paper.

"And, lad? Here's a little something to encourage

the old man to pay the bills." The man passed a dressage whip through the window. Alex noticed right away that it wasn't the modestly priced version he'd brought up to the counter. It was the best whip in the store.

The man turned, walked over to a low-slung green Jaguar, and drove away.

"Well," Meredith demanded. "What does it say?"

Alex unfolded the piece of paper.

"Limestone Farm. There's a phone number."

Alex

THREE DAYS LATER Alex rode down a long driveway shaded by towering fir trees and lined with sword ferns and waxy salal bushes. The forest opened out onto a field and the sky reappeared over the winding gravel road, which wound down to meet a lake.

Turnip walked briskly, and his head swung from side to side as he took in the unfamiliar sights. He had an old gelding's well-honed sense of self-preservation and was not one to get excited unnecessarily. When a big bay horse galloped up to the fence and snorted a challenge, Turnip gave it a sidelong glance of cautious disapproval and moved on. As always, Alex felt proud of his horse's steadiness and solid common sense. He gave the old paint a pat on his neck.

Alex was still in shock at the warm, friendly greeting the man had given him when he finally gathered the courage to call the number on the card. The man, who said his name was Fergus, had promptly invited him to come for a lesson.

"I, uh, don't have a horse trailer," said Alex, feeling like the whole thing was too good to be true.

"And where do you live, lad?"

Alex explained and Fergus laughed. "I think you're in luck. We're not too far from you." He gave Alex the name of the road and Alex realized it was only about a fifteen-minute ride from his place.

"Think you can make it that far?" asked Fergus.

"Oh, yes. Definitely."

Now that he was on his way to his first dressage lesson he could hardly believe it. *It's like heaven here*, Alex thought, eyeing the house and outbuildings and the lake beyond. Motion in an outdoor ring caught his eye.

It was a horse and rider at the end of a lunge line. The bald man from the store stood in the middle of the circle holding the line, which was clipped to the horse's bridle, and a long whip that he wiggled to tell the horse to go forward.

Alex was familiar with lunging. Meredith had kept him on the end of a lunge line when he was learning how to ride. Alex remembered that riding in a circle on the end of a lunge line while someone else controlled the horse made it easier to focus on his seat and position. He'd lunged Meredith's horses, riderless, to exercise them and warm them up. But he'd never seen an experienced rider on the end of a lunge line and the girl in the ring obviously knew how to ride. She wasn't using reins or stirrups and was basically maintaining her position. That couldn't be easy—Alex could see that every stride the horse took was basically jet-propelled.

"Relax your hips," said the man.

As she got closer, Alex could see air between the girl's seat and her saddle. A whisper of nerves prickled across his neck. *What if he was terrible at dressage?* If this girl, who obviously had all the advantages money could buy, was having trouble with her riding, what would happen to him? He'd hardly even been in an English saddle before. *What if Meredith was wrong? What if he had no talent?* He wished Meredith had been able to come with him for his first lesson, but she was busy packing.

"Walk," said Fergus. The girl began to tip forward.

"Sit back! Shoulders open."

"Shit!" said the girl, and Alex suppressed a gasp. Meredith would have killed him if he swore during a lesson.

When the big mare finally slowed to walk, the girl slumped over in her saddle.

"God," she said. "I totally need a chiropractor."

"What you are going to need is an attitude adjustment before Ivan gets his hands on you," said the man. Then he noticed Alex and Turnip.

"Hello, dear boy!" he called.

Dear boy. The man had called him *dear boy*! Alex felt his smile widen.

"So you've found yourself some English tack."

Alex nodded. Meredith had lent him an old close-contact saddle and helped him cobble together an English bridle from bits and pieces she had lying around. The new mismatched English gear didn't suit Turnip particularly well. In fact, Alex found himself very aware of the stark contrast between Turnip and the horse in the ring. It wasn't just a matter of height—the two horses could have been different species entirely. Alex mentally apologized to Turnip for his disloyal moment.

"Wonderful. We're going to have a lot of fun. Isn't

that right, Cleo, love?" said Fergus.

Cleo slumped over on her horse, lolling her head theatrically. "I guess that depends on how you define fun." In that moment, Alex recognized her as the dressage rider, the girl he'd seen at the fall fling.

"Okay, you can get off now. I think you've had enough for one day."

"Thank God," said the girl, displaying all the energy and grace of a wet dishrag as she slid off the tall mare.

"Another beautiful dismount, Miss Cleo," said Fergus, still not showing any sign of actual irritation. "Now remember, when you finish untacking Tandava and cooling her out, you're to clean all her tack and then you've got her stall to clean."

The girl, who was petite and had delicate, almost sharp features under her black riding helmet, rolled her eyes.

"Please tell me you're kidding," she said. "I'm paying full board. What's with all the work?"

"Your parents are paying, darling. Big difference. Students at Limestone work. It's part of the dressage lifestyle."

"No wonder I'm your only student," grumbled the girl.

"It's only been a few days, my dear. We've barely gotten started with you. And this young man here may be our second student. I don't want you scaring him off."

Alex wasn't scared. He was intimidated, but so excited he would have whipped off his shirt and started scouring the barn floor with it if asked.

"Good luck," said the girl to Alex as she drooped her way out of the ring. He could tell she didn't recognize him from the horse show and he was relieved.

"Come on in," said Fergus. Alex jumped off Turnip and led him in.

"So who is this fine gentleman?" asked Fergus, walking around Alex's horse.

Alex felt a twinge of embarrassment. "His name is, uh, Turnip, Colonel Turnipseed."

He pushed away his desire to make excuses for his horse. Turnip might not be the fanciest horse around, but he was definitely the smartest and bravest. And the most patient.

"Let's have a look at you ride, shall we?"

Alex swung easily back onto the old paint and began to move him around the arena at a walk, then a more ground-covering trot, which kept slowing to a Western jog. He had to remind himself to post rather than sit. The stirrups were too short and the little saddle felt odd. Alex barely touched Turnip's sides, and the horse broke into the ultraslow lope that is the hallmark of a good Western pleasure horse.

"Okay, Alex, bring him back to a walk and come in here a second," directed Fergus.

Alex slowed Turnip and turned him to the center of the ring so he faced the small man.

Fergus gently patted Turnip's neck with a flat hand. "Well, he's just a love, isn't he?"

Alex nodded, relieved the man wasn't making fun.

"He's got quite good balance and a good mind. I can see that right off. Not a big mover, of course, and you aren't that familiar with the English tack. But I'm sure we can do something for you and your root vegetable. First, however, we're going to have to rustle you up a dressage saddle. This one has you tipping forward like a jockey."

Alex tried to contain his huge smile. He nodded quickly again and looked down at his horse's mane instead of giving away his ridiculous, outsized happiness.

Alex

AS HE WAS struggling out of his track pants by the side of the road, Alex reflected that two weeks of dressage training had turned him into a master of disguise as well as a liar. Well, not a liar, exactly; he was really more of an omitter. He didn't need to tell everyone his personal business, even though lately it seemed that everyone was interested.

To pay for his lessons, he'd worked out an arrangement with Fergus in which he cleaned stalls and helped out around the farm, fixing fences, driving the tractor to harrow the ring, and picking out paddocks. He was at the barn every day after school and most of Saturday and Sunday, but he still hadn't quite gotten around to telling his father that he'd switched from Western to English.

"So, who you going to train with now that Merry's gone? She was a damn fine little horsewoman, that one. It'll be tough to replace her," his father had commented last night.

Alex had mumbled some vague reply about taking lessons at a place down the road.

"They do reining there? Because I think that's the natural progression for you. You've shown you can do that slower-type stuff. It's time to work on your speed. I was talking to Rudy Chapman down at the Wheat Sheaf, and he said . . ."

Alex tuned out. Rudy Chapman was a man who specialized in rough-handling problem horses. If you wanted the spirit knocked out of your horse, Rudy Chapman was your guy. If you wanted somebody to drink with while talking trash about horses, he was also your guy. If Alex's pants were on fire, he wouldn't have taken Rudy Chapman's advice on where to find a water hose.

Alex wasn't one to confront issues head-on. That's why he didn't argue with his dad or tell him the truth. Instead he kept his English tack at Limestone, telling Fergus he felt safer riding over in his Western gear. He left his house wearing baggy track pants over his breeches, the same track pants he was now struggling to get off. Twice today he'd been caught by passing cars as he hopped around on one leg by the side of the road before the turn-off to the barn. The elderly female driver of the first car, obviously afraid to see what he was doing with his pants half down, sped up after giving him an alarmed glance. The young aboriginal guy driving the second vehicle had grinned widely, and given him the thumbs-up.

He had one leg free and was working on the other when he heard another car approach. *Damn*. He crouched closer to Turnip, who stood solidly in place. The car, which sounded mechanically suspect and familiar, slowed as it got closer. Alex stayed very still, his half-removed sweatpants lying in the dust as he hid behind his horse at the side of the road.

"Alex?" came his aunt Grace's voice.

Alex swore silently under his breath and peered out past Turnip's shoulder. The gelding gently lipped at his hair.

"Do you mind telling me what the hell you're doing?" Grace's hair was extralarge today, and boldly highlighted. She looked right at home in the car—an IROC with a damaged muffler and a fat white racing stripe running up the middle of the hood—that Alex's dad had from before he was married. Grace drove it around the neighborhood to her home hairdressing visits. It was, Alex thought, the ultimate white-trash vehicle.

"Nothing. Getting changed."

"Into what? Your Superman cape?"

Alex sighed and straightened.

"Those are quite the pants you've got on there," Grace said, noticing his breeches as he pulled off the other leg of his track pants.

"They're for riding," he said.

"If you say so. Anyway, I'm off to do Nancy Ferguson's hair. She broke her leg at the curling club dance, so she's not getting around much."

Grace revved the engine a couple of times. "Please don't take off any more clothes by the side of the road. You never know who's going to stop. Oh, and don't worry. I won't mention this to anyone." Then she jammed the car into gear and roared off.

Alex breathed a deep sigh of relief. Grace understood the need to be discreet. Alex knew his father was eventually going to find out he'd switched to dressage, but there was no need to rush.

Mr. Ford had definite ideas about the merits of Western versus English riding. He referred to

Western as "real riding." Traditional Western mounts, such as quarter horses and paints and mustangs, were "real horses." English was "fancy riding" done by "sissy riders" with "useless horses."

Mr. Ford was also a big believer in the power of the cowboy hat. He often said that any man could succeed with the ladies if he had the right ten-gallon. Alex politely refrained from mentioning the right ten-gallon could probably get a guy quite a few other guys as well.

When Alex and his sisters found their father passed out in his lawn chair outside his RV, they all pitched in to get him to bed, but rarely spoke about it afterward, other than to make veiled references to it.

"Keep an eye on the lawn chair," Grace would tell Alex before she went out if it looked like his father might not make it up the stairs.

Alex and the twins almost never brought friends home, in case the "lawn chair" was having a bad night. But loyalty mixed with shame kept them from confronting their father about his drinking or anything else. The atmosphere around his house was thick with secrets kept at bay with jokes.

Alex's *tendencies*, as he had come to think of certain feelings, were another family secret. He wondered if his aunt and sisters knew or at least suspected about him. He still had a faint hope that his desires would cooperate, or at the very least that he could keep them under wraps until he was out of high school. Alex didn't exactly deny who he was. He just tried to ignore it in the hopes that it might die of oxygen deprivation.

The few openly gay guys he'd met, mostly his aunt's friends, seemed to him to belong more to the girl world, the world of hair and clothes and makeup. Alex's heart was in the world of men—mighty steeds and fireman hats—the land of cowboys. That didn't mean, however, that he wanted to *be* a cowboy. What Alex wanted, more than anything, was to be like everybody else.

He wasn't certain what to make of his new coaches, two men who apparently lived together. His solution, as usual, was not to think about it.

Ever since he was little, his interest in things male had been, well, exclusive, but he still told himself that he might develop a desire for or interest in girls. When he was being honest with himself he knew that since "it" was as deep in him as his heart, he wouldn't.

Everyone seemed to understand the situation, at least on some level. Everyone, that is, except Cleo O'Shea, who was still the only other student at Limestone Farm. Cleo made him nervous, so he was constantly flustered around her. For some reason, she interpreted this as some kind of pathetic attempt at flirtation on his part.

At first Alex had been intrigued by Cleo. She was the first truly wealthy person he'd ever met. He'd always assumed that someone who'd grown up wealthy would be cultured and sophisticated. Instead Cleo was profoundly shallow and spoiled in a way he'd never seen outside of television. She not only *looked* thirteen, she acted it.

Cleo O'Shea was quickly becoming the one thing he didn't like about dressage lessons. She was always *talking* to him—talking *at* him. Telling him private things about herself. She came early and watched his lessons and followed him around as he worked, talking the entire time. Talking, talking, talking. But never, ever working. She talked more than both his sisters and his aunt put together, and incredibly, she worked even less.

That voice of hers was like a squeaky windshield wiper.

"Are you hanging out with anyone special, Alex?"

He'd evaded her questions, but later the same day as his aunt caught him changing by the side of the road Cleo tried a new tactic.

As Alex switched Turnip's tack back from English to Western for the ride home after his lesson, Cleo came and stood in the doorway of the barn.

"Oh, hi, Alex. You heading out now?"

He muttered something unintelligible as he tightened the girth. Cleo fidgeted, shifting her weight from foot to foot, and picked at her riding gloves.

"Mrs. Mudd isn't here yet to drive me back to school. So I'm just waiting around. Anyway, I was thinking maybe we could hang out this weekend."

Was this lunatic female asking him out?

"Maybe we could go to a movie or something," she continued.

Excuses flapped through his mind. Sick . . . aunt visiting . . . terminally ill . . . don't date . . . don't date girls . . .

It was time to bring out the big guns. He should have done it sooner. Time to unleash his Secret Imaginary Girlfriend, also known as the Certain Special Someone.

"Well, I might be seeing my, uh, girlfriend. The

one I'm, you know, dating."

Alex used a white-haired girl he'd met at Pentecostal Bible camp as the model for his Secret Imaginary Girlfriend. All he remembered about her is that she'd smelled of wet bathing suit and of the LePage's glue she consumed in large quantities, and he'd envied her terribly because at home she had an Appaloosa named Spot.

"You have a *girlfriend*?" asked Cleo.

He nodded quickly. "Yeah. She's got an Appaloosa. Its name is Spot. You know, because it's an Appaloosa."

No need to mention that he hadn't seen or spoken to his white-haired, glue-smelling girlfriend since he was eleven.

Cleo considered this for a moment, her face pensive. Then she said, "Well, that's okay."

Alex couldn't believe it. *Was she a sociopath? How dare she bulldoze her way past the Secret Imaginary Girlfriend! The nerve!* He searched his mind for more excuses.

"I've got this family thing, too. So I'm pretty booked," he added.

Cleo looked disappointed again, but not disappointed enough. Alex could tell from her expression that she wasn't going to be deterred by a fictional family thing or by a Secret Imaginary Girlfriend. There had to be something he could do to get her to back off. The barn was his refuge and he planned to keep it that way.

7

Alex

CHRIS AND SOFIA arrived just as the lesson was ending. Alex hoped that he'd be doing something impressive when they showed up, maybe an extended trot or at least cantering, but no. He was at the end of a lunge line, like a little kid just learning to ride.

When Alex saw Cleo being lunged, he'd approved of the idea. For her. He was certain *he* wouldn't need any help with his seat and balance. Fergus informed him otherwise at his second lesson.

"You have a good seat, dear boy, but we need to challenge it. You don't mind being lunged?"

Alex shook his head no. He figured it would take Fergus about three seconds to see he didn't need remedial help and they could head right into the advanced stuff: piaffe, passage, pirouettes, and the other grand prix movements.

It was not to be. At each lesson Alex was lunged both on Princess and Turnip. He was lunged until his spine compressed and he developed a bobble head. He was lunged until the insides of his legs bled. Still, Alex couldn't decide whether to be embarrassed or excited about the process. He'd read somewhere that riders at the Spanish Riding School in Vienna spent *three years* at the end of a lunge line before they were ever allowed to take up the reins. He felt thrilled to be part of such a demanding tradition. The other part of him felt that even though he was new to dressage anyone who loved it as much as he did should be a natural, especially if that person had been riding seriously since he was twelve.

"Yes, but you rode Western," Fergus said when Alex mentioned his concerns. "Now you have to learn a dressage seat. I'm not saying you don't have a good seat. You do. We're just fine-tuning it."

The other way Alex knew he wasn't a dressage prodigy was because Ivan hadn't come out to give him a lesson yet. Fergus had told them that Ivan would only teach him and Cleo when Ivan thought they were ready.

Part of the challenge for Alex was the difference in horses. He was used to riding horses that had been trained to be as comfortable as possible. Riding Turnip was a little bit like being aboard a nicely upholstered couch. Riding Princess, however, was like standing on the deck of a small boat in choppy water. Every stride threatened to send Alex flying. The more tired he got, the worse his balance became. By the end of his lessons he felt like he was bouncing around like a first-time rider at a dude ranch. That's what was happening when Chris and Sofia showed up.

After Fergus told him he was welcome to invite people to watch his lessons, he'd invited his friends out. His hope was that Cleo would mistake Sofia for his girlfriend. He hadn't told Sofia the plan, however, and he couldn't invite her and *not* invite Chris. So now they were both here and he was left wondering how his nicely compartmentalized life had gotten so messy.

From the corner of his eye he saw Chris and Sofia walk over to the ring. Like many unhorsey people in an equine environment, they looked worried that someone would suddenly ask them to hold a rearing stallion or put on a rubber glove so they could help a mare give birth.

Alex wanted to play the gracious host but it was hard from the end of a lunge line. He satisfied himself with nodding at his friends, but suspected the gesture was impossible to make out amid the head wobbling.

Fergus ignored the new arrivals and kept talking to Alex.

"We have to work on your flexibility. You've got to let go in your hips. Even at the walk you need to feel that pelvis move!" he announced in a loud voice.

Alex stared off into the distance like a sick dog. He knew what was coming next.

"I want you to imagine you are *making love* to the saddle."

Fergus, standing in the middle of the ring, began to move his hips like a geriatric Chippendales dancer.

Oh, please, oh, please, let him stop doing that, thought Alex. He snuck a glance at his friends. Sofia was definitely grinning.

"It's about freedom and strength," said Fergus, swinging his hips back and forth. "Freedom here!" Fergus put his hands on his hips like he was about to begin the "Time Warp" dance. "And strength here and here!" He vigorously slapped his belly and then his own rear end.

Alex saw Sofia duck her head behind Chris to hide her laughter. This wasn't what he'd had in mind at all. He felt a little better when he saw Chris smile encouragingly at him.

"Okay. Once more to trot."

Screw it. The damage was done. He might as well finish his ride properly.

Alex sat deep and tall, making sure there was a straight line from his hip to shoulder, and looked ahead through Princess's ears as he urged her forward. He let his hips absorb the movement and Princess responded by rounding and softening her back. All at once Alex was floating.

"This is it!" cried Fergus. "You feel this? How she's swinging through her back? Now you are really sitting! Okay, now you ask for the walk just by slowing your seat and tightening your stomach muscles."

Alex did as instructed and Princess slowed to a walk. It was the best moment he'd had so far in his dressage training. He smiled, his embarrassment forgotten.

"Riding this way is not easy," said Fergus, still speaking loudly, as though he intended his words to be overheard.

"Your horse, he is trained in Western pleasure. He

tries to make you comfortable by moving as slowly as possible. In truth, he barely moves! A horse like Princess is something else again. You have to meet her halfway, or sitting on her is misery. But look at you. Two weeks and already you're having some very nice moments."

Alex glanced over at his friends and saw that they, too, were smiling and he was no longer sorry that he invited them.

Twenty minutes later Alex had Princess in the cross ties. He'd finished hosing her down and scraping off the excess water.

"So this one's yours?" Sofia hesitantly patted Turnip's soft white nose, which poked out of his stall.

"Yeah," Alex said. He felt tongue-tied around his friends in this unfamiliar environment.

"I can tell he totally loves you."

Startled, Alex glanced at Sofia.

"He watches every move you make," continued Sofia.

"He's a really good horse," said Alex. His throat felt too closed up for him to say more.

"This place is incredible," said Chris, who'd taken off his headphones and was investigating every inch of the barn. Chris had an artist's fascination with the physical world, and Alex surreptitiously watched as his friend trailed slender fingers over the wood and brick surfaces. Abruptly, Alex looked away. It was bad enough when straight people developed friend crushes. For a gay guy to get a crush on his straight friend was practically suicidal.

Sofia came over to give Princess one of the carrots she'd brought.

"I wish someone would do all this for me," said Sofia as she watched Alex massage Princess's neck.

Alex, a careful person to begin with, was even more meticulous than usual when he worked on Princess, who accepted his attention as no more than her due.

"Maybe you should talk to Alex about that."

Chris, Sofia, and Alex all turned to see Cleo standing in the doorway.

Alex felt his jaw tighten. The plan had been for Cleo to meet Sofia and just *assume* Sofia was his girlfriend. Cleo wasn't supposed to *say* anything about it.

"You're just how Alex described you," said Cleo, walking up to Sofia, with her hand outstretched.

Alex blinked. *Was she on crack?* He hadn't said word one about what his girlfriend looked like.

Cleo stopped in front of Sofia. Her handmade riding boots were spotless for once. Her butter-yellow breeches glowed, and her white blouse was freshly pressed. Her small chin jutted defiantly and her sheer pink lip gloss gleamed softly in the warm lights of the barn.

"How was your ride?" she asked Alex after she finally let go of Sofia's hand.

"It was fine," he replied. He picked up one of Princess's front hooves. He'd cleaned it already but needed something to do. He would spend an hour cleaning each hoof if that's how long it took Cleo to go away.

Cleo's next question took his breath away.

"Do you mind competing for his attention with a Turnip?" she asked Sofia.

"No, not really," said Sofia with an uncertain laugh. "A rutabaga, though—that would be a different story."

Alex's back began to hurt as Princess shifted more of her weight onto him, but there was no way he was going to straighten up while the two girls were talking.

"That's funny," said Cleo. "I just wondered how you as Alex's girlfriend feel about how, you know, *horsey* he is."

"I don't know. You'd have to ask Alex's girlfriend."

"You mean you're not . . . ?"

"Not that I'm aware of."

Alex's back went into a spasm. Reluctantly he let go of Princess's foot and stood.

Alex's eyes met Chris's. Almost against his will Alex said, "Uh, I'm not going out with my, uh, girlfriend anymore. We broke up, I mean, it didn't work out."

That evening Alex was exhausted, not just from his lesson and the chores he'd done at the barn, but from all the messy and terrifying social interactions. It was almost a relief to get to work cleaning Turnip's stall.

He hurled the last clump of sodden shavings into the wheelbarrow and was pushing it out of the stall when he nearly ran into his father.

"What the heck's going on in here?" asked his father in his beery baritone.

"I didn't hear you come in," said Alex, picking up the shovel in a half-hearted gesture of explanation. Then he was hit by a sinking feeling. He'd forgotten to put his track pants back on. He was still in his breeches. Maybe his dad wouldn't notice. He sounded fairly plastered.

His heart sank when his dad leaned against the stall, settling in for a visit.

"It's Friday night," said Mr. Ford. "And here you are. Shoveling shit. There'll be time for that, son, after you get married."

"Yeah. Ha, ha," said Alex.

"Jesus," said Mr. Ford. "What kind of pants you got on?"

"Riding pants?" Alex replied, hoping that was all the explanation his dad would need.

"They look like them funny English pants the girls wear."

Alex didn't respond. His mouth was so dry he couldn't swallow, much less speak.

"Why you wearing them sissy pants?" Mr. Ford persisted.

Alex felt like one of those captive-raised game birds that people let out just long enough to shoot.

"I've been, uh, riding English. At a place down the road."

"English?" said his father, screwing up his face with distaste. "I thought we talked about this. You were going to look into roping or reining, maybe working with Rudy Chapman—"

Oh dear God, thought Alex, *not Rudy Chapman again*.

"I've decided to try dressage," Alex said in a quiet voice.

"Dressage?"

"You know. It's English. It's kind of like . . ." Alex struggled for a way to describe the sport. He couldn't use the dancing analogy, because that would make things worse. The only thing his father would hate more than a son who rode dressage was one who danced. "Dressage is sort of like military riding," he said finally. "It's a style of classical riding that was developed hundreds of years ago for war horses. For soldiers. You know that musical ride that the Royal Canadian Mounted Police put on? That's basically dressage. Dressage comes from the word *dresseur*—to train. It's—"

"I didn't ask for a damn seminar," his father interrupted. "What is it? What are you going to do with it?"

Alex blinked.

"I don't know. Compete. I guess."

"I thought only girls do that dressage stuff. Going around and around in circles like that."

Alex briefly considered taking the shovel and stabbing himself through the heart with it.

"Lots of men ride dressage," he said. "Some of the top riders are men. Especially in Europe."

"Yeah, and I bet most of them are a little light in the riding slippers, if you get my meaning," said his father, twinkling his fingers at Alex as though trying to put him under a spell.

"Yeah, well, I'm not," Alex said, and he knew his voice sounded a bit high-pitched and defensive. This would all be so much easier if he was a misunderstood straight boy, like that Billy Elliott kid. Lucky bastard.

"Did you ever think all this riding, especially this fancy dressage riding," Mr. Ford said, adding another finger twinkle for emphasis, "is getting in the way of a healthy social life?"

Alex suppressed a shudder. What did his father know about a healthy social life? His main form of entertainment was drinking himself into a stupor alone in his RV every night.

"How you going to meet a girl when you spend all your time with your horse?" his father continued.

"Dressage is practically all girls."

"Never see any of 'em around here," said his father.

Alex was about to point out that between his sisters

and his aunt the place was practically overrun with females.

"It just don't seem *right*," his father continued. "Take your old man, for instance. I'm a hardworking guy. Not much time for socializing. And even I find time to see the odd lady."

Alex's stomach heaved.

"You even met the lucky gal I'm taking out tonight. Remember Colette?"

So his father *was* dating the woman from the beer garden, she of the sparse red hair and unused dressage horse.

What could Ms. Reed, a successful realtor, possibly want with his father? Mr. Ford's skin was puffy and yellowish, but he was all dressed up in a nice shirt and khakis and had doused himself in some god-awful cologne. The old man was probably ripe for a massive heart attack. He could go at any moment. Running a business *and* a family into the ground had to be very hard work. The old man deserved some happiness.

"You're dating Ms. Reed?" Alex said finally, trying to work some enthusiasm into his voice.

"One of the men in this family has to get a little action."

Alex's mouth took off on its own before he could stop it. "Don't worry. I'm seeing someone, too."

"That right?" His father sounded surprised. *How dare he sound surprised!*

"Yeah. This girl from the barn. She goes to Stoneleigh, actually." *What was he talking about? Why couldn't he shut up?*

"Well, you old dog, you," said his father, smiling.

"She's cute. Rich, too."

Mr. Ford beamed. Then he chortled, "Don't get her knocked up."

He must have seen Alex's horrified look because he tried to explain. "Your grandpa. That's what he used to say to me every time I went on a date."

"That's, uh . . ." Alex struggled to find the right description. "Good advice."

"And the other thing your grandfather always said to me was, 'You want I should get you some protection?' He always said it with an Italian accent. Even though we weren't Italian." Mr. Ford's voice was wistful at the memory.

Alex felt himself start to sweat. Was his dad about to give him the dreaded Talk? Or worse, some protection? Was he going to hand over a condom, warm from his pants pocket, *a condom meant for Ms. Reed*?

"That's great, Dad."

His father looked at Alex searchingly.

"I mean I don't need any protection," Alex clarified.

Mr. Ford laughed, then stepped closer and clapped him on the back.

"Okay, son," he said. "No protection for you."

Cleo

"CLEO O'SHEA—you have a phone call on the common phone."

All the girls in the TV room looked over at me, surprised. The bitches. But I was already out the door, headed for the phone alcove.

On Friday nights the academic girls study in their rooms or hang around the library. The horse fanatics clean tack or brush their horses or something. The party girls sneak out and go into town. The rest of us watch TV. I am seriously considering becoming a party girl, just for the stimulation and because we never watch the shows I want.

The only person I can relate to at all in the Friday TV–watching crowd is Phillipa. I've been feeling sort of bad about leaving her to train with Svetlana while I go off to Limestone. I've been surprised by how much I miss riding with her. Phil's pretty easygoing and much more agreeable than Alex. Lucky for him that he looks like a model for an Eastern European clothing line, or I might get tired of his attitude.

"Hello?" I said, breathless from my dash to the phone.

"Uh, Cleo?"

It was him! I'd done it! I'd used my powers to will him to call. Sometimes I amaze even myself.

"Yes?" I said, pretending I didn't know who he was.

"Hi, it's Alex. Um, Alex Ford. You know, from the barn."

"Oh, *Alex*," I said, loud enough so anyone listening would hear. Too bad he has one of those androgynous, could-be-a-boy-or-a-girl names. "*Alexander*. Hi!"

He sounded nervous—that was *so sweet*.

"Yeah, so I'm, um, free on Saturday," he continued. "If you still want to get together."

I *knew* he liked me. Girls have instincts about these things.

I considered saying I had to check my schedule, you know, making him sweat a bit. But I couldn't. I was totally accepting this date.

"Great," I said.

"So you're free?" His voice dipped almost like he was disappointed. Maybe I should have made him wait.

"I think so. But, uh, not till later." That's it—I would play hard to get. But only moderately hard to get, as opposed to extremely.

"Later?" he asked.

Why later? How much later? Why was I such a spaz? You'd think I was from around here or something.

"Like not midnight or anything. But not early. We have dining hall at six. So how about seven?" Was seven o'clock later? I didn't even know at this point. I was starting to lose it.

"Okay."

"Why don't you come here? Pick me up. Then we'll go to your place." I wanted everyone to see me with him. To see me with any boy, actually, but especially one with big, sad eyes and curly brown hair.

"On second thought, how about you pick me up

at six-thirty? That's probably better for me," I said.

Alex was quiet on the other end of the phone. Finally, he gave this defeated little "Okay," like I'd just told him he had to put his cat to sleep. I did not understand the tone of that "okay" *at all*.

"Great! See you then."

I hung up the phone and began jumping up and down and making the V for victory sign in the hallway.

I know Alex is the guy who's going to help me redeem myself in the romantic department. I am perfectly capable of having a *normal* relationship with a nice, noncriminal guy who likes me for myself, no matter what my parents say.

Alex

ALEX DIDN'T LIKE Cleo, at least not *that* way. So why was it taking him so long to find something to wear? He had to look nice, but not so nice that she would be overcome with lust. Alex had had a dread of uncontrolled female desire ever since that incident in the third grade when Lucinda Watts got him alone in the music room and asked him if he wanted to go steady. Lucinda had skinny arms and legs and large, rubbery lips that she slathered with sparkly pink Lip Smackers. When he turned her down, she kissed him anyway.

Thinking of pink goo, he put on his third-choice outfit and made his way downstairs to the kitchen to get Grace's and his sisters' approval.

As Alex came down the stairs he heard Grace say, "Maggie, I recognize that as a young teen you have a lot on your mind, but have you ever considered the effects your sallow skin may be having on your self-esteem?"

"We aren't sallow," answered May, because Maggie was too busy constructing a fake wound on her arm to reply. "You told us so that time you put the cloth around our heads and pretended we were bald."

"Yes, but I'm more educated now and I've decided your skin tone is sallow. It's just your luck that I have a new cream that will revolutionize your life by helping with jaundice."

"You mean that medical makeup you got for people who are getting chemo?" asked Maggie, finally looking up from her wound making, the tubes and jars and brushes for which were scattered all over the counter across every inch of space that Grace's cooking mess hadn't already taken.

"That's what the cosmetics are *designed* for," said Grace. "But they work well for other people, too. I need to practice before I go putting them on someone who might be a bit irritable due to having a touch of cancer or kidney failure or whatever."

"I think you should just focus on your cooking," said Maggie. "And cleaning your hand."

As part of her new passion for all things East Indian, Grace was attempting to cook vegetarian Samosas. Earlier in the day she'd henna'd one of her hands very badly. It looked as if she'd cut it off and left it outside on the lawn by itself all summer.

May stared at the purply red blotches on Grace's hand.

"You should've done a foot," she said.

"Then you could put a sock over it," said Maggie.

"You might want to consider wearing a glove on that hand," said May.

"A silver one, like Michael Jackson!"

"You could tell people you have that skin disease that makes you look white!"

"I am white. Unfortunately. You two have no sense of appreciation for other cultures," said Grace, fiercely stuffing fresh herbs into mashed potatoes.

Alex cleared his throat at the doorway. Three heads swiveled around.

"The suit was too much," said Maggie.

"But a tracksuit is too little," finished May.

"It's not a tracksuit," Alex explained. "It's casual wear."

"Alex, it's a tracksuit," said Grace. "I can see the Adidas symbol. What are you—the missing Beastie Boy? Where are you taking this girl, anyway?"

Alex cringed. This was all such a charade. He felt as though someone had installed a neon FRAUD sign on his forehead.

"If you both ride horses, why don't you wear something riding related?" suggested Grace.

"Breeches?"

"No, cowboy stuff. You were the cutest little cowboy," said Grace, dropping one of the Samosas on the kitchen floor. She absently picked it up and put it back on the tray. Alex made a mental note to avoid the Samosas.

"He can't wear cowboy clothes. He rides English now," said Maggie.

"Dressage," said May, looking very satisfied with herself. "He's gone back to his first love. Dressage riding."

"Just remember you have to drop us off at the dojang first," said Maggie.

"And pick us up," said May.

"And make sure the *N* is on the car to warn everyone else that the world's least experienced driver is behind the wheel," said Grace, fishing around under the counter for another fallen Samosa.

Alex slowly climbed back upstairs to his room, where he decided on an outfit of jeans and a blue shirt and sweater. Then he went outside to put the *N* for novice driver symbol on the car. The IROC was the least appropriate vehicle possible for someone who liked to wear sweaters. He was sure a little part of him died every time he had to drive it. And now he had to drive it to the most exclusive private school on Vancouver Island.

Five minutes later the twins emerged from the house. He watched through the rearview mirror as they staggered along under the weight of various swords, gloves, mouth guards, and long and short sticks. They pulled open the sticky passenger door, pushed forward the front seat, and piled themselves and all their equipment into the backseat.

"One of you can sit up front," he told them.

"Actually, you can drop us off *after* you pick her up," said Maggie.

"What?"

"We'd like to meet her."

"And we don't have to be at practice right away," said May.

Alex cranked his head around to look at his

younger sisters crammed in the backseat behind a bristling fence of weapons. They grinned at him. Alex considered arguing with them but they were too heavily armed.

"Shouldn't you have all that, you know, *weaponry* in a bag or something? What if we have an accident?" On second thought, having an accident wouldn't be so bad. It would save him from having to go through with this date.

"F.E.I.," said Maggie, whose grasp of acronyms was weak, "Grace took our equipment bag to that hairstyling competition on the mainland and it never came home."

"Oh," Alex said, then started the car.

He drove the rumbling muscle car around the RV as slowly as possible, nervous even though his father's truck wasn't in the driveway.

"Don't worry. He's not home," said May.

"I think he's out with that rich lady again," said Maggie.

"Have you *seen* her?" asked May. "She needs Hair Club for Men like no woman I've ever seen."

"She's rich, though," said Maggie. "I'm hoping she'll want to adopt us. I think it would be a good move for us financially. If she does adopt us, I'm going to ask for a motorcycle."

"My guess is that we'll be too busy holding Ms. Reed's hand at her hair transplant surgery for you to have much time for motorcycles," said May, who was more practical than her sister, but not much.

"I bet the doctors could take the hair from Dad's chest and graft it onto Ms. Reed's head!" mused Maggie. "Then Grace would just have to dye it."

"What's that smell?" asked May, who wasn't one to give much notice before changing subjects.

Alex didn't answer. His rapidly intensifying headache made speaking seem like a bad idea.

"Is that Stetson?"

"Lawdy, lawdy," yelled May, "Hawg ain't a cowboy no more, but he sure smells like one."

Alex hunched lower in his seat and put on his signal for the turn coming up a mere half mile away.

In spite of their offer to accompany him, Alex left the twins in the car and walked to Stoneleigh's main building by himself. He slowly followed the woman who answered the door down the hallway. The floor was old linoleum and the dull green wall paint looked like it dated back to the 1970s. Stoneleigh might be a private school for the wealthy, but it was dowdy.

"I can wait here," Alex protested, as the plaid-skirted woman with swollen ankles and hair in an untidy bun started to lead him into the dining hall.

"That's fine, dear. Cleo asked me to bring you right in." The woman lowered her voice and leaned in, bathing him with her cigarette breath. "I think she wants to show you off."

She pushed open fake wood-paneled double doors to reveal a cafeteria that seemed to be on the edge of a riot. Girls' voices and laughter and shouts and shrieks echoed around the room. Dishes crashed and scraped, and cutlery clanked. The place smelled like boiled hot dogs and old gerbil cages.

After she opened the door, Alex's escort stepped aside, leaving him completely exposed. A sea of dark-blue school sweaters shifted, and a hundred, two hundred, a thousand heads turned to look at him. There, in the middle, sat Cleo—a patch of bright green—*Dear God, what on earth was she wearing?*—in a sea of navy-blue school sweaters. The cafeteria went quiet.

From where he stood, Alex saw a little smile curl onto Cleo's lips. She made no move to get up.

He started to panic. She had another thing coming if she thought he was going to impersonate

Richard Gere in *An Officer and a Gentleman* and stride over and carry her out.

Luckily his heavy-ankled escort took pity on him, perhaps sensing that he was about to cut and run.

"Miss O'Shea. You have a visitor," she announced.

Slowly, Cleo rose from her seat, causing her green paisley blouse to billow and ripple around her. She wore a very small white denim skirt. It looked like she'd raided some family's closet and had the mom's clothes on top and the little girl's clothes on the bottom. Head held high, she moved toward the door.

"Hey, O'Shea—you forgot your tray!" said a long-faced girl with brown hair, smirking at the other girls at her table.

Cleo turned, grabbed her meal tray, and set it firmly down in front of the girl who'd spoken.

"Drop that off for me, would you, Bronwen? I've got a date."

Then Cleo, finally smiling, strode to meet Alex. And in that moment, Alex felt like he could love Cleo O'Shea.

The feeling only lasted until Cleo got in the car, or rather until Cleo threw herself into the car. She must have been a little keyed up, because she nearly hit the roof when one of the twins gave a discreet little cough in the backseat. Cleo twisted around to stare at the twins. Alex suddenly saw his sisters through Cleo's eyes: two identical females with brown hair in tangled ponytails, wearing white pajamas and carrying . . . knives? Swords? Sticks? Weaponry of some kind. He considered being embarrassed, but then decided he was too tired. He fit the key into the ignition and the IROC's engine resisted once, twice. On the third try it turned over and roared to life.

Maggie leaned forward and stuck a hand over the seat at Cleo. "Hi, I'm . . ."

Her voice startled Alex into remembering his manners.

"These are my . . ." he said, raising his voice over the engine, so that he was almost shouting.

"Hi, I'm . . ." bellowed May.

"You must be . . ." yelled Cleo.

"Maggie."

"Sisters."

"May."

"Alex's sisters."

"I think I saw you guys at a horse show once," said Cleo, cranking her head around. "I just didn't realize you were Alex's sisters."

"That's because we're allowed to roam freely over a wide area," said May. "But we are available should a situation arise," added Maggie mysteriously.

"I'm sorry, I didn't catch that," said Cleo.

The twins' reply was lost beneath the roar of the car's engine as Alex drove slowly out of the Stoneleigh parking lot.

Cleo

I CAN'T PRETEND I wasn't weirded out. He brought his sisters. On a date. And they were *armed*. Was Alex Ford from a military family or something? I wasn't even aware that Canada *had* a military. I thought they were one of those pacifist countries. Like Switzerland.

I considered asking Alex about Canada's military, you know, so he'd think I was one of those people who is interested in other countries. I'd keep it quiet so the junior commandos-in-training in the backseat wouldn't hear and think I was stupid, but then I noticed that driving, even at tranquilized granny speed, took all of Alex's concentration. It's a good thing he doesn't ride like he drives. I may have had a driver most of the time, but I do know *how* to drive, which is more than Alex can say.

Then there was the issue of his car. Now I know why he rides his horse over to a barn for lessons. The noise alone would be enough to send Tandava through a fence. The car doesn't suit him at all. I may not know him well enough to make those kinds of judgments, but the whole point of our date was to fix that. If we hook up I'm going to advise him to get a new car.

"So you ride with Alex?" yelled one of his sisters from the backseat.

"Yeah," I said.

"But isn't Stoneleigh a girls' riding school or something? Why don't you ride there?"

I turned to answer and then realized that my seat belt had pulled open my shirt so that my bra was showing. When I bought it I thought my shirt looked sort of peasant chic, but now I think it makes me look more homeless and color blind than anything else. I tried to be subtle about pulling it closed, but I didn't need to worry. I could have stripped naked and Alex wouldn't have taken his eyes off the road. He looked straight ahead as if the street were lined with improvised explosive devices or something. His white-knuckled hands gripped the steering wheel at precisely ten and two and he seemed afraid to shift, maybe because that would have meant taking his hands off the steering wheel. The engine screamed as we roared along in low gear.

"They mostly teach jumping at school," I yelled back. "I ride dressage. Same as Alex." The noise from the engine was brutal.

"Do you think maybe you should shift?" I asked him.

Alex didn't react. The left-hand turn signal had been on for at least three blocks.

"Dressage, dressage, dressage," said one of the twins in an exaggerated French accent.

The other one joined in. "Passage, piaffe, renvers."

I turned around, thinking they were laughing at me.

"Sorry," one of them apologized. "It's just that when Alex was little he used to wander around muttering those words to himself."

I glanced over at Alex. He was ignoring all of us.

"Dressage, half pass, *oui*?" said a twin.

"*Piaffe et volte et dressage*," said the other one.

"You speak French?" I asked, just to be polite. It

was pretty obvious they didn't know French.

"We like to think we speak dressage."

We drove from Yellow Point, where Stoneleigh is located, into downtown Cedar, which basically consists of a baseball field across from a mini-mall.

I looked around as we drove and it occurred to me that there was a good chance Alex was a have-not. I knew he wasn't rich or anything, but I thought he'd be at least middle class. What if he lived in one of these falling-down trailers? What if his mom was one of those hugely obese ladies who can't fit out the front door of her double-wide and wears a stained housedress and eats Cheetos all day? What if his dad has no teeth? I quickly practiced my not-horrified face so that I wouldn't betray my real feelings when we finally got to his tar-sided shack with the inbred, handicapped chickens flapping around in the dust outside.

Suddenly one of the twins shrieked, "Left! Oh my God! Left! Alex—turn here! *Now!*" which scared Alex so much that his foot came off the gas, the car stalled, and we coasted silently into a pothole-filled little parking lot.

"Good thing you have that *N* on the rear window,"

said one of his sisters as Alex brought the car to a stop in front of a plain white building with a garage on one side and a small doorway on the other.

"It's a good thing he's a better rider than he is driver, eh, Cleo?"

I saw my chance to score points.

"Oh, he is," I gushed. "He's a really great rider."

We all sat in silence for a few seconds.

"Uh, you're going to have to move so we can get out," said one of the twins.

"Sorry," I said as I scrambled out of the car and pushed the seat forward.

"Imagine if someone attacked Alex for his bad driving," said one twin as she tried to push some of her weapons out the door, "and they forced him off the road so they could give him a beating."

"That would be so cool," said the other one, who was trapped behind a wall of swords and sticks. "At first they'd think he was a tough guy because of the car. Then they'd see that he's all sweaters and cords and rubber boots. So they'd be like, 'Let's get him. He's a gentleman farmer! He's no threat.'"

"Yeah! They'd try to pull him out through the front window by his hair."

"Only we would pop out of the backseat where

we'd been hiding. We'd come flying out like ninjas!"

At this point, they were both still trapped by their equipment but seemed too busy babbling about their violent fantasy to notice. Alex sat with his head resting on the steering wheel.

"The guys wouldn't believe their bad luck for picking the deadliest car in all of Cedar. Maybe even all of Nanaimo!"

"Yeah!"

Still talking about the epic beating they were going to inflict on their brother's fictional attackers, the twins finally freed themselves and piled out of the car, half their gear clattering to the pavement as they went.

"See you at nine-thirty!" said the one wearing a camouflage-patterned terry-cloth headband. She and her sister flashed supersized grins at Alex and me as they disappeared into the building. I got back into the car and shut the door.

The car seemed very quiet without them.

After Alex dropped off his sisters he drove us back to his house.

"Are you sure you don't want to go to a movie, or something?" he asked.

I was all, *No, no, that's fine. We can hang at your house. Even though your mom probably weighs 450 pounds and your dad weighs 80 and has no teeth and lost his job at the chicken manure factory a while ago and hasn't gotten back on his feet since.*

I was all geared up to show him that I have no problem with poor country folk. Still, I was pretty relieved when we stopped at a regular-type house. In Cedar, people with lots of money live right next door to people who have none. The Fords' place was somewhere in the middle. Their house was big and fairly new, your basic white box. They must have some money because they had a speedboat parked in the driveway and a trampoline on the front lawn, and a huge motor home, the kind used as dressing rooms on movie sets, parked right beside their house.

Inside, the house was messy. Seriously messy. Alex could have had a 450-pound mother buried somewhere under one of the giant piles of clothes that lay everywhere and no one would ever know. Also, from what I could see beneath all the clothes, the decorating was tragic. Somebody had a major jones for homemade dried-flower arrangements and pictures of sad-eyed clowns.

"Don't take off your shoes," said Alex, when I

went to bend down. "I haven't had a chance to do the floors."

He hadn't done the floors? I'm not one of those insensitive Paris Hilton types who thinks every family has help, but didn't his mother do the floors?

"It's the girls' week to do laundry. They haven't quite gotten around to folding yet," he said.

Or picking it up off the floor, I thought.

I followed him through the living room, and all the sad clown eyes seemed to follow us. The kitchen was airy and bright and even messier than the living room. It was occupied by a woman in her twenties who had the biggest hair I've ever seen.

"This is my aunt Grace. Grace, this is Cleo," said Alex.

"Have a Samosa," she said, like she was giving me an order. She seemed to be in the middle of some sort of severe ethnic identity crisis. She wore a bright blue sari with silver trim. A bindi had fallen off her forehead and was stuck in her eyebrow.

"You made these?" I said, trying to give the impression that I was impressed. Alex's aunt made his sisters look practically normal. She wasn't quite as well armed, but her hands—or one hand, anyway—was absolutely filthy, disgustingly, revoltingly dirty—and she was offering me food with it.

No wonder Alex seems to like cleaning stalls so much. Horses are models of cleanliness compared with his aunt and sisters.

"Well?" Grace asked, impatiently shaking her giant hair so that the three or four shades of noncomplementary highlights shimmered. "Do you like it?"

I looked around for someplace to hide the Samosa. I considered dropping it down the gaping hole at the front of my shirt, but I knew it would leave a big telltale grease trail.

"I'm a superdomestic person," said Grace, staring at me. "I love my career as a hairstylist, but I would also jump at the chance to have my own cooking show." As she spoke the bindi fell out of her eyebrow and landed precariously on her chin.

I tried to catch Alex's eye, but he seemed lost in thought as he stared out the window.

Realizing I was going to be forced to taste the brown lump, I took a deep breath and raised it to my mouth. I was shocked to discover that it actually tasted good. I took a second bite. It had some kind of curry mixture inside. On the third bite something pierced the roof of my mouth.

"Ow!" I said, and then tried to cover with an

"Mmm." I began feeling around the roof of my mouth with my tongue.

"Can you taste the rosemary?" asked Grace. "I picked some from one of the flowerpots outside the courthouse when I was paying my parking tickets. At least, I think it was rosemary."

"I, uh . . . ," I said. "There's something . . ." I opened my mouth and pointed inside.

"Oh, damn. Did you get a splinter?"

I nodded, my mouth still open.

"Would you mind getting it out, Alex?" Grace said, unconcerned that her food had just attacked me. "It took me like half an hour to get that last one out of May's mouth. In the meantime, I've got about a hundred more Samosas to deep-fry."

She reached over and grabbed up a pair of tweezers resting on a piece of tinfoil butter wrapper. "Here, use these."

I stared at the tweezers. No way was anyone getting near me with those things—not even Alex.

"Come on," he said, tugging at my dangling peasant sleeve.

For a moment, I forgot the pain. He touched me! Well, he touched my sleeve, anyway. I was halfway to having a regular, noncriminal boyfriend who was my age. Man, when I put my mind to something, I amaze even myself.

I started to get a little concerned when Alex didn't lead me into a bathroom or a nearby surgical unit, but headed outside. We walked into a field where Turnip stood near the gate, watching us with that slightly quizzical look he always has.

I told myself this was normal. Lots of dates end up in a barn or, you know, some other private space. I was probably just experiencing nerves due to the pain of the splinter and anxiety about the health implications of possibly having those nasty tweezers in my mouth.

I stood in the doorway of the small two-stall barn while Alex turned on the lights. The little barn wasn't fancy but it was spotless and perfectly organized. There wasn't a stray piece of hay on the floor. It smelled of fresh shavings and leather. Alex fiddled with something at a small worktable.

"Thith is tho cute," I said, lisping due to the pain from the rosemary barb. "I mean the barn. It'th really nithe." I didn't say it was nicer than the house, even though it was.

"Don't worry. I won't use the tweezers Grace gave me," he said. "We don't want you to catch some flesh-eating disease. I just want to make sure mine are sterilized." He pulled a pair of tweezers from a large plastic first-aid box. He opened the bottle, poured some of the contents into the plastic lid, and dipped the tweezers into the liquid. Then he wiped them off with a fresh piece of paper towel. Watching him took my mind off my pain. His movements were so precise and *careful*.

He turned and walked over to me. He was tall enough that he could look into my mouth when my head was tilted up.

"Grace's food is almost always spiked with something. Bottle caps, pieces of tin," he muttered as he peered into my mouth. "Sorry, I should have warned you."

I gave an embarrassed laugh, because he smelled nice and he was looking in my mouth and I felt like a moron.

"Darn, I can't find it. Come in here," he said. "The light's better."

I followed him into a brightly lit tack room. He sat me down on a bench that ran the length of the room. He leaned in close so he could look into my mouth again.

I'm not sure if it was relief or something else that

made me feel so dizzy when he finally pulled the splinter out.

"Thanks," I said, feeling around the roof of my mouth with my tongue to make sure it was gone.

"No problem," he said, smiling down at me. Maybe it was gratitude or maybe it was the way his smile was so unguarded and genuine. All at once I knew I was crazy about Alex and his messy house and his tacky car and his weirdo family. He was this little spot of sanity in all the chaos and I wanted him to be my sane spot. *I* wanted to make a mess in his life so he could clean it up in that very deliberate way of his. It's hard to explain, but the feeling was overwhelming. There was only one way I could express it. Without thinking, I half stood and abruptly kissed him.

He pulled back so fast that he banged his head on a saddle rack behind him. I was left standing there, half crouching, with my lips all puckered up and my hands sort of clawing at him. I froze in that position and from my peripheral vision I saw that my stupid peasant blouse was hanging open and my bra was showing again. I didn't know what to say, so I muttered, "I'm so sorry," as I stood and tried to adjust my shirt.

He seemed to think I was making another move on him because he jumped away, banged his head again, and shouted, "Gay!" at me.

"What?"

"I'm gay," he said, holding up his hands like he was ready to fight me off if necessary.

I have never been so embarrassed in my whole life. I collapsed onto the bench. Then I decided *I* had to get away, so I tried to get up again so I could leave.

He threw out a hand, like a traffic cop stopping an aggressive driver. I sat back down. He was starting to piss me off.

"Jesus. Would you relax already? I was just trying to stand up."

"Oh. Okay, then," he said, then slumped down onto the bench beside me.

Neither of us spoke for a minute. We just sat there. In the quiet, I had one of my rare moments of actually considering how someone else might feel. Alex just came out to me, and all I could think of was to be embarrassed by my lack of gaydar and my totally inappropriate sexual advances.

"I'm sorry," I said again. "I guess I'm not . . ." How was I supposed to finish that sentence? What could I say that wouldn't be offensive?

"A guy?" he said.

It was the first joke I'd ever heard him make. Was it just my imagination or did he suddenly seem more relaxed now that he knew I wasn't trying to assault him?

"I should have known," I said.

"Why? I didn't exactly, you know, tell you."

We were interrupted by a noise outside. I heard a vehicle pull up and car doors open and close, then the voices of a man and a woman. The man's voice was deep and the woman's was sort of raspy.

The voices came closer. I looked over at Alex and saw that his face had gone pale. He glanced at me quickly as the voices came closer, as though he wanted to say something, but before he could speak a man stuck his head in the door.

"Well, if this don't beat all!" said the man, who had short dark hair and was quite handsome in that square-jawed sort of way really big guys sometimes are. He looked like Alex, only coarser. His face was flushed, like he'd been running or maybe drinking.

He stared at us nearsightedly from the doorway, until he was joined by a lady with violently red hair, an obvious dye job. You could tell she was a bit older than the man. I figured she must be Alex's mother.

"Well, well, well. Who have we got here?" asked the man.

The lady smiled. Her lipstick was electric against her pale skin.

Alex stared at the far wall.

"Hi there," I said, giving them this little wave, which instantly made me feel like a dork. "I'm, um, Cleo."

The man gripped the doorway and the redheaded lady gripped him.

"Pleased to meetcha, Carrie," he said. As he spoke I caught a whiff of his breath. He hadn't been running.

"Brian, shush!" the lady stage-whispered. "She said her name was Chloe. Or something." Then she giggled.

"Good going!" said the man, giving Alex an exaggerated wink.

"Cleo, this is my dad," said Alex in a dull voice.

When Alex didn't introduce the lady, his father spoke up.

"And this here's Colette Reed. I'm sure you've seen her face on bus shelters and billboards around town. Colette's a famous realtor in these parts," said Mr. Ford. "This guy treating you all right?"

The lady didn't seem to like him paying attention to me. She grabbed one of Alex's dad's arms and clasped it to her chest. "That is a very *unusual* blouse, honey."

Ooooh! I wasn't going to let her get away with that.

I grabbed Alex's arm and held it exactly the same way Colette Reed held his father's, and said, "Yes, sir. Alex definitely knows how to treat a girl."

From the corner of my eye I caught Alex's smile as he stared back down at the floor.

PHASE II

Riding the collected horse in turns and circles at all paces (in America commonly called "gaits") and in perfect balance. This is known as the Campaign School. . . . The proficiency and stamina of the horse will be increased, his intelligence and understanding awakened, and the rider is given a line of conduct to be followed for further training. . . .

This second phase of riding has to be developed from the first and presents the only possible preparation for the third, namely the High School. Only on this foundation can the rider proceed to art, that is, to High School, because nature can exist without art, but art can never exist without nature.

—Alois Podhajsky, *The Complete Training of Horse and Rider in the Principles of Classical Horsemanship*

11

Alex

ALEX TRIED TO stay calm but it was difficult. Today was his first lesson with Ivan and he felt as if a pro scout had come out to watch his minor league match.

"Don't be nervous," Fergus told him, right after giving him the news that Ivan would teach his next lesson. "He's gruff but he's brilliant."

Gruff didn't quite capture it, thought Alex as Ivan strode into the ring. Terrifying was probably a more accurate description. The tall, white-haired man stopped in the center and crossed his arms high on his chest as he watched Alex warm up.

He's probably only ever taught elite riders, thought Alex. *He's going to think we're crap.*

"As I was telling you earlier, Ivan, Alex has just come off the lunge line. He's been riding his Turnip and our Princess. He has a very nice, natural seat and quiet hands," said Fergus.

"Alex, my dear. Would you please take up the reins and go over your basic paces on the root vegetable."

For the next ten minutes Alex walked, trotted, and then cantered Turnip. Fergus asked him to do ten-, fifteen-, and twenty-meter circles, loop serpentines, and figure-eights. Ivan watched, his face betraying nothing.

"Okay, this is enough," he said as he waved Alex into the middle of the ring.

Alex wiped the sweat off his forehead with the back of his glove and gave Turnip a pat.

"This horse is how old?" asked Ivan.

"We don't quite know," said Alex. "My dad got him from someone."

"I'm thinking he has a big heart," said Ivan. Something about the way he said it made Alex's own heart lurch in his chest. "He tries very hard but I'm thinking this is not for him.

"I'm thinking he's sore. It's hard for him to go forward. He's stiff in the hocks and the left shoulder.

Maybe age, maybe too much work, too young."

Fergus nodded his agreement, and his usually cheery face was solemn. "That's what I was worried about. Alex, you must have noticed he's been getting stiffer since we started lessons."

Alex had noticed but he'd tried to convince himself that Turnip was just getting used to using different muscles. Now the truth was out. His dressage training was over practically before it had begun. "So I can't ride anymore," he said. He could feel heat prickling at the backs of his eyes.

"Not this horse. He'll be trying for you, but it will cost him too much." Ivan's stern face was gentle for once. "I'm sorry. You have no other horse?"

Alex shook his head. There was no way he could afford to buy or even lease another horse. And he would never sell Turnip. The horse was his best friend. His savior. He knew his face was flushed. Suddenly he had to get out of the ring. He heard a scraping noise and looked over to see Cleo opening the gate and leading Tandava in for her first lesson with Ivan. The mare's dark coat shone like polished mahogany and her step was light. The sight of them made Alex feel even more heartsick.

"Okay. Well, thanks," he said. He swung down

off Turnip. "I'll leave the saddle in the tack room."

"We'll think of something," Fergus called after him, but Alex didn't stop. He couldn't. He ignored Cleo's quizzical look as he walked quickly past her. All he wanted was to jump on his horse and gallop away as fast as he could go, just like he used to. But he couldn't even do that anymore.

Grace found him in Turnip's stall.

"Alex?" she said, peering over the half door. The gelding's head was lowered so it nearly rested on Alex's shoulder. Alex had been sitting on the footstool in the corner for an hour and a half.

"What are you doing in there?" Grace asked.

"Nothing," he said, wishing she would go away and leave him alone.

"Alex, you're hiding in your horse's stall. You only do that when you're upset."

"I'm not hiding."

"You can't keep secrets from your auntie Grace. Come on now."

He shook his head, afraid that if he told her what had happened he'd start bawling or something.

Grace opened the door and slipped into the stall with him.

"They said Turnip can't do dressage."

"Who did?"

"My coaches. Fergus and Ivan."

"Why not?"

"That guy who had him before me probably didn't feed him properly. Worked him too hard when he was young. He's fine for trail riding. You know, he's not lame or anything. He just can't do anything too demanding. Like dressage."

"Damn," she said, sliding down to sit with her back against the wall. "You really like those dressage lessons."

"I like lots of things," he said. "That doesn't mean I get to do them."

"Actually, I'm not sure how many things you really *do* like," said Grace. "This dressage stuff seems pretty important to you. I guess I can see why. From the little bit I've seen it's cool in an uneventful sort of way. Cleo said you have a lot of talent."

Neither of them spoke for a minute or two. Then Grace changed the subject.

"Your dad's over at Ms. Reed's," said Grace.

Alex shrugged. Lately his dad was always at Ms. Reed's, at least when he wasn't sleeping one off in his motor home. In a way it was a relief. Alex hadn't had to pry him out of his lawn chair for weeks. With Mr. Ford always at Ms. Reed's, it was even easier to avoid thinking about him than when he was in his trailer.

"Didn't you tell me once that Ms. Reed has a dressage horse?"

Alex was surprised that Grace remembered. He'd forgotten Ms. Reed's invitation to ride her horse. She stopped offering after she'd bagged his father.

He nodded slowly.

"I think we should go talk to her. See if she'll still let you ride it. Especially if it does this dressage stuff."

The thought of having anything to do with Colette Reed made him feel vaguely queasy. But not as queasy as the thought of giving up dressage.

Grace put a hand on his shoulder and pushed herself up. Then she reached down for his hand.

"Come on, Depresso. I know she's a little scary, but you won't be riding her. Unlike your—"

"Stop!" said Alex. "Don't say any more."

"See? I knew I could take your mind off your troubles. You want to drive or you want me to?"

"Can we walk?" asked Alex, as he brushed past his aunt on his way out of the stall.

"What? And miss the opportunity to make the IROC backfire? Where's your sense of adventure?"

Alex had never actually been to Ms. Reed's house. She didn't seem interested in getting to know her new boyfriend's family. Once Alex had seen her standing awkwardly in her red high heels outside the motor home, waiting for his father. Alex and his sisters and Grace had been on the deck having a late fall barbecue and Ms. Reed kept shooting them insincere little smiles.

"You sure you don't want to come in here and wait, Colette?" Alex's father had called from the trailer.

Ms. Reed shook her head quickly, as though living in an RV might be contagious.

"You're welcome to join us for a barbecued soy patty," said Grace from the deck.

"We've got ketchup," said May.

"And mustard," added Maggie as further enticement.

Ms. Reed grimaced at them.

It seemed to Alex that she found the reality of her new boyfriend's life distasteful. Or maybe she just didn't like motor homes and veggie burgers. Either way, when Alex's father emerged from his trailer, reeking of aftershave, she lost no time in heading back to the truck.

"You sure you don't want to join the kids for a bite?" Mr. Ford asked.

She didn't even bother answering. She just got in the truck and slammed the door.

"I don't think she's going to be over here cooking Sunday dinner anytime soon," Grace said, watching them drive off.

"Thank God," muttered Alex, visualizing Ms. Reed in one of her all-one-color business suits with an apron on top, clicking around their kitchen in her matching high heels.

Ms. Reed's acreage was neatly fenced with split rails. The shrubs and ferns surrounding the house were tastefully chosen and well placed. The paved circular driveway was swept clear. Mr. Ford's big black truck and Ms. Reed's champagne-colored Lexus were parked in front of the house.

When Alex got out of the IROC the first thing he did was look around for a horse, but he couldn't see one.

"Do you think she still has the horse?" he asked nervously.

Grace shrugged and dumped the keys into her big green purse. "She'd better. We're not visiting for nothing."

Alex saw a small building at the end of the pasture that he thought might be a barn.

"Maybe it's in there."

Alex and his aunt stood side by side in the driveway, staring at the house, which was sided in cedar and had large windows all the way around. Alex saw someone move inside.

"They're in there," he said. "We should knock or something."

"Shit," said Grace, who seemed to be losing her nerve.

"Come on," he said, leading the way to the front door.

He picked up the heavy iron knocker and let it fall.

There was a rustling inside, then scraping and a click as a lock turned and the door slowly opened.

Ms. Reed's eyeliner was smudged into the wrinkles beneath her eyes. Her red hair was flat in several places, allowing her pink scalp to shine through. It was three o'clock in the afternoon and she wore a floor-length purple paisley dressing gown with gold satin trim and a gold belt.

"Yes?" she said.

"Uh, hi, Ms. Reed."

Ms. Reed squinted at him suspiciously, as though he were a Jehovah's Witness going from door to door.

A shuffling, clomping noise came from inside the house and then the door opened wider.

"We don't want any— Son?" said his father, who was bleary-eyed but didn't look quite as destroyed as Ms. Reed. At least his father was dressed.

"Hi, Dad," he said.

"Alex? Grace?" said Mr. Ford. "What are you doing here?" Concern came into his eyes. "Everything okay with the girls? Did something happen to Darlene?"

"Darlene?" asked Ms. Reed. "Who's Darlene?"

"His wife," said Grace. "My sister."

"Ex-wife," clarified Alex. "No, it's not Mom. It's nothing bad. I'm actually here to see Ms. Reed. Uh, Colette."

Ms. Reed still looked suspicious that he was going to try to give her some copies of *Watchtower*.

"You mentioned once that you had a horse. A dressage horse. You said you were looking for someone to ride him," said Alex.

Ms. Reed frowned. "That's right, I have a horse."

Alex waited for her to say something else but she didn't.

"I'm sort of looking for a horse to ride."

"What's wrong with your Turnip?" asked Mr. Ford.

"He's getting older. It looks like he might have some arthritis or something."

"Damn good horse," said Mr. Ford to no one in particular. "Alex here put a lot of training into that horse. Did real well on him at the local shows."

Ms. Reed looked from Grace to Alex to Mr. Ford and Alex could see her mind calculating. Finally she said, "I suppose it wouldn't hurt Detroit to get some exercise."

"I take lessons," said Alex. "At a barn in Yellow Point. It's really close to here. If it's okay with you I could take your horse over there for lessons."

Ms. Reed smacked her lips together and then stepped back and picked a highball glass off a three-legged table. She took a deep drink, then handed the glass to Mr. Ford. She pulled him close after he finished the last of the liquid. "I'm sure that would be just fine," she said, batting her eyes at Alex's father.

Alex felt his excitement rise. "That's great. Can I

meet him? Your horse?"

"Sure," she said distractedly. "I think he's over there. In the barn. My barn girl is off today, so I suppose that's where he is."

With the interview over, she moved to shut the door.

"Bye, son," said Mr. Ford as the door closed.

The first thing Alex noticed was the unmistakeable smell of an uncleaned barn. The next thing was that the barn was in near-total darkness because no lights were on and the day outside was overcast.

"Help me find the lights," Alex said as he felt around one side of the doorway.

Grace moved to search the other side. She must have found the switches and flipped them all at once because the lights above flickered and suddenly the entire barn was ablaze with bright fluorescents.

"He must be in there," said Grace, pointing toward a closed stall door with bars across the top. Alex was already on his way. When he reached the stall door and looked in, he found the horse facing the back wall, its backside toward him. It stood fetlock deep in its own filth.

The barn was spacious and looked nearly new but

the horse inside seemed to be almost an afterthought.

"Hey, fella," said Alex softly.

The tall bay horse wore a nearly new blue rug but the blanket was smeared with manure. When the horse finally turned around, Alex could see its eyes blinking painfully as it tried to adjust to the light.

"Grace, can you turn off the light in his stall?"

Lights flicked on and off overhead as she tried to figure out which switch controlled the stall. Finally she hit the right one and the stall went dim again.

Alex saw most of a flake of hay uneaten on the filthy floor and an automatic waterer in the corner. At least Ms. Reed hadn't forgotten to feed her horse.

"Come here, fella," said Alex, pulling open the door a few inches, then reaching out a hand for the big bay horse to sniff. Slowly the horse's head moved forward until Alex felt whiskers tickle his palm. He stroked the horse's nose and cheek and saw that the animal's eye, now that it had adjusted to the light, had a kind expression. Alex stepped out of the stall and grabbed the nylon halter hanging from a hook.

"You sure?" asked Grace.

Alex nodded. "He'll be okay. He just needs to stretch his legs."

Seconds later Alex had the halter buckled onto the horse's head and was sliding open the stall door. He braced himself in case the horse came charging out—after all, he'd been shut in for who knows how long. But the horse waited politely for Alex to lead him out of the stinking stall and put him in the cross ties.

"He's huge," said Grace.

The horse *was* big. Alex figured he had to be at least 16.3 hands. "Okay, big guy. How about we clean you up?"

"If you're going to brush him, I guess the right thing would be for me to clean his stall," said Grace.

"It's okay," said Alex. "I can do it."

"No, no," said Grace. "It's the honorable thing. You brush the big guy and I'll take care of it."

Alex slipped off Detroit's blanket, revealing a very well-built but out-of-shape dark bay horse. As he did so, he heard his aunt dig through her purse, open her cell phone, and punch in a number.

"Hi, May? Yeah, we're over here at Ms. Reed's."
Pause.

"Looking at her horse. For Alex to ride."
Another pause.

"You don't want to know. Anyway, I want you and

Maggie to get ready. I'm coming to pick you up. Why? Well, Alex needs some help over here."

When she finished the call, Grace walked past the big gelding, who was stretching out his neck and wiggling his bottom lip with pleasure at being brushed.

"Okay, so I'll be back in ten minutes with your sisters. They'll clean the stall while I hide from Ms. Reed. How does that sound?"

Alex turned to his aunt and smiled. "Good. And Grace?"

Grace turned around in the doorway.

"Thanks."

It was her turn to smile. "*De nada*, my friend," she said. Then added, "That's Spanish, in case you were wondering."

Then she left Alex to the wonders of the new horse.

Cleo

IT WAS ALMOST the end of November when I came back from classes to discover I'd been assigned a roommate. She was lying on my bed in her riding boots.

"Hey," she said.

"Uh, hello?" I put a somewhat offended spin on it so she'd at least move her feet.

"This your bed?" she asked, staring up at the ceiling, her legs crossed at the ankles.

"Yes." Going for extremely offended now.

"Mind if we switch? I don't like facing north."

"North is that way," I said, pointing at the wall beside her.

"You know what I mean," she said.

A disorganized pile of what I presumed were her belongings lay in a heap in the middle of the room. Half of it was spilling out of designer luggage. The other half was hanging out of plastic orange garbage bags. She obviously wasn't one of those organizational geniuses I keep hearing about. I could see from the insignia of the coat that lay on top of the pile that she was part of the senior jumping team. The team is a very big deal here at Stoneleigh. They compete all over western Canada and even in Washington and Oregon. Two girls who used to be on the Stoneleigh senior team are now on Canada's national team. Another girl recently made the American equestrian team.

Well, I wasn't about to give this bed-lying boot-wearer all kinds of respect just because she had a team jacket.

"Look, I think there's been a mistake. I'm not supposed to have a roommate."

"You are now," she said, smiling sleepily at me.

"I don't think so. My mom arranged it so . . ." That sounded too lame. "I mean, it's part of my deal. Double room, no roommate."

"I'm Jenny," she said. "I believe you have been assigned the job of keeping me on the straight and narrow for the rest of the school year." She turned up the wattage on her smile. Her teeth were large and square and white. The rest of her was large and tanned.

"I'm Cleo," I said. "And I really think you've made a mistake."

There was no way they'd give me a roommate, especially not one from the jumping team. Those girls stick together, and they have a reputation for being wild. They are a completely different species from dressage riders. I think they've all got the low cortical arousal thing that extreme athletes suffer from. You know, they have to do dangerous stuff just to feel alive. Personally, I feel most alive when I'm watching TV or reading. Or sleeping.

I noticed a yellow sheet of paper with the Stoneleigh logo sitting on my desk. It was a room transfer form assigning Jennifer Hillier to Room 132. My room.

My disappointment was overshadowed by my interest. Why had Jenny been moved? Was this some kind of punishment? What had she done to get herself exiled to *my* boring room? Was I really supposed to be a calming influence?

I cleared my throat. "So, what brings you to my room?" I asked and immediately felt like kicking myself, because it sounded like a lame pickup line.

It didn't matter, though, because Jenny had fallen asleep. I heard a faint, whistling snore.

"Narcolepsy, huh," I whispered to myself. Then I started making up my new bed.

My situation at school isn't the only part of my life that's changing. Things at the barn are upside down, too. When I first moved Tandava to Limestone Farm, my riding got better immediately. Fergus was teaching us, and he's one of those people who makes everything fun. It didn't seem to bother him when I complained. It never bothered me when he nagged. I was happy. Tandava seemed happy. She was no longer threatening to blow up every time I got on her. In fact, she was starting to go pretty well because Fergus lunged me so much that my seat improved. That meant that my horse didn't have to worry so much about me accidentally jerking her in the mouth. She softened up and relaxed, and I had moments when I could feel why she cost as much as she did.

But then Fergus decided Alex and I were both ready to take lessons from Ivan. That brought the fun to a screeching halt. Ivan doesn't tease when you make a mistake. *Au contraire!* He says extremely rude things, which I don't appreciate.

The only thing that makes it tolerable is that Ivan really knows what he's talking about. He's gotten on Tandy a few times, and each time I've been amazed. She seems to grow five inches and every beautiful thing about her gets more beautiful when he rides her. She arches her neck and her steps get longer and her shoulders freer. Even her coat looks shinier. Ivan rides like he was born on a horse. He sits very still and quiet and Tandava listens intently when he whispers to her in Hungarian or Bulgarian or whatever it is he speaks. In some ways Ivan reminds me of Alex: Alex has that same presence on a horse, the same total focus that horses respond to.

The difference is that Ivan is a bitter, bitter man. Why else would he make me do all that backbreaking physical labor? Like cleaning stalls for horses that aren't even mine, cleaning my tack after every single ride, and picking up crap in the fields and paddocks. You'd think I wasn't a paying customer. And if I do the slightest thing wrong, Ivan loses it. Once I brought Tandy into a lesson and she had a few pieces of hay in her tail. He went all WMD on me. "This is disrespectful to your horse! To me!" he said. Then he kicked me out of my lesson.

I worry that if Alex keeps up with his undercover, Mr.-Secretly-Gay-Guy-Who-Only-Hangs-Out-With-Horses routine, he's going to end up just like Ivan, a bitter old man in a pirate shirt.

Alex and I have been hanging out a lot lately. I think our friendship is really deepening, but he's quite shut down. For instance, if I want to go over to his place, I have to invite myself because it would never even *occur* to him that he wanted company, even though I know he does. Also, he's extremely humorless about his family situation. I know his dad lives in an RV and has a little drinking problem and a balding girlfriend, but as far as I'm concerned, that just adds color. I tried to tell Alex that but he just snorted. Like a horse would.

He avoids his sisters and his aunt Grace, who are extremely entertaining. It's like they're too messy for him, even though their messiness is what makes them so great and funny. I worry about him, I really do. He's missing out on life. One day, when we were at the barn, as usual, cleaning tack after our lessons, also as usual, I tried to talk to him about it.

"Do you think that your secretiveness about your sexuality might be holding you back?" I asked.

He looked at me like I'd suddenly kicked a small, defenseless animal across the room.

"What?" he said.

"You could be experiencing resistance in your riding and your personal life because you are resisting your own inner truth." Actually, I knew he wasn't experiencing much resistance with Ms. Reed's horse, but it sounded good.

Fortunately Alex didn't call me on the weaker part of my argument.

"My own inner truth," he repeated in a flat voice.

"Totally. Don't you worry that your self-denial is affecting your riding and your development as a human being? I really think you've got to get past your fear and come out."

He gave me a sour look and went back to polishing the silver snaffle, which already gleamed like a piece of jewelry.

"Don't get defensive. I'm not telling you to wear assless chaps to school or anything. I just think your family—well, your aunt and sisters, anyway—would be cool with it. Then you could have a more open life. You need to let people in."

"First," he muttered, "all chaps are assless. That's how they're made. And second, there's more to my family than my aunt and my sisters." He reached over to take the bridle I was supposed to be cleaning. I guess I was so busy helping him to sort out his issues, I forgot. I handed it to him.

Before I could argue my point, which was strong, Fergus walked into the tack room.

"*You*"—Fergus pointed at me—"are not to let *him* do your chores."

"But he doesn't like the way I clean things."

"I'm sure he'll cope."

"But he always redoes everything after I finish."

Fergus made a dismissive noise. "You, little minx, will clean up after yourself so Felix Unger here doesn't need to fuss." He took the tin of saddle soap from Alex's hand and put it down beside me on the bench. "Here you go."

"Felix Unger?" said Alex, after Fergus had left.

"I don't know. Must be some classical reference, like from James Joyce or something," I said. "Hey, what are you doing later? I thought I'd stop by your place."

13

Alex

ALEX WAS, AS usual, worrying. He sat in the IROC waiting for Cleo to finish saying good-bye to his sisters and Grace and worrying that he was wasting valuable time. She always insisted on stopping at his house on the way home from the barn and it took hours to drag her away. He wished he'd never told her that he'd drive her home from Limestone Farm so she didn't have to catch a ride with Mrs. Mudd.

The other thing he was worried about was the news Fergus had dropped on them after their lesson that afternoon. Fergus announced that Alex and Cleo would be riding in a clinic with a trainer from Europe who was an old friend of Ivan's. The clinic instructor had done his training at the

Spanish Riding School.

The Spanish Riding School! Just to be in the presence of someone trained at the finest and oldest dressage school in the world was an honor Alex could scarcely comprehend. Then his nerves and pessimism kicked in.

Colette Reed's gelding had turned out to be a very well-schooled midlevel dressage horse. Fergus and Ivan estimated that he was probably trained to at least third or fourth level. He had his flying changes down and was able to do beautiful, floating extensions and solid collected work. Luckily Ms. Reed had barely ridden the horse, so she hadn't ruined his paces or his willingness.

Detroit had been living at the Fords' for a few weeks. Alex suspected that Ms. Reed had allowed him to take her horse home because the move had given her an excuse to drop in unexpectedly on his father.

Detroit's main problem was that he was out of shape and starved for attention, so Alex spent hours gradually building his stamina and reintroducing him to the world. Soon after Alex moved Detroit to his place, he began using Turnip to lead Detroit to and from his lessons at Limestone Farm. He knew he was a strange sight riding along in Turnip's Western saddle in his breeches and tall boots. In rainy weather he wore his Australian outback oil slicker coat and covered both horses in brightly colored rain sheets. Cleo said it looked like Crocodile Dundee had gone on a rampage in a J.Crew outlet store. Fergus said it was a miracle the spectacle hadn't caused an accident on the road between Cedar and Yellow Point, but so far Detroit had been calm and steady and willing to follow Turnip's lead.

Perhaps because of the lack of stimulation at Ms. Reed's, the big gelding had a habit of staring long and hard at new objects. In each new setting he went into a kind of reverie, gazing around and moving very carefully. He reminded Alex of a man who'd just regained his sight. The thing Alex found most amazing was that the horse was at least as good-natured as Turnip.

"Perhaps it has something to do with the handler," said Fergus.

Even Ivan was impressed at how well Alex and the new horse were working together. "You're patient. You give the horses confidence in themselves. This is good." Alex hoped his coaches were right, that he did help his horses believe in themselves, because he wasn't at all sure he believed in *himself*.

Fergus must have seen the doubt on Alex's face at the announcement because he said, "Don't worry, lad. You'll be just fine. And you too, lass, provided you focus and don't mess around."

Alex wished he could believe Fergus. He sometimes wondered if his coaches were just nice to him because they felt sorry for him. He worried that he was talentless and they were afraid to tell him because they knew dressage was all he had.

On the drive to his house, Cleo had tried to cheer him up.

"God, don't be such a dark cloud! It's going to be great. The Spanish riding guy will love you. And me, obviously. I've been in lots of clinics with these big-time trainers and they're nothing to worry about. Some of them are kind of cranky, but who cares, right? It's just a lesson. It's not the Olympics or anything."

It was easy for Cleo. She didn't have to worry about anything. As Alex sat in the IROC waiting for Cleo, he arranged everything in the glove box and carefully wiped down the dashboard and stick shift and fretted that he could be doing something useful like reading *Dressage Today* or memorizing a new dressage test or watching dressage videos.

Alex argued with himself constantly about Cleo. He liked her but she was just so spoiled and opinionated. He knew she meant well with her advice, but what did she know about anything? All the girls who attended Stoneleigh had money, but Cleo was rich even by their standards. Her parents produced movies and her father was some famous director who, according to Cleo, specialized in making very boring movies set in foreign countries.

Cleo had once casually mentioned that her house in Los Angeles had eight bedrooms, even though only she and her parents lived there. She'd grown up with a nanny and a live-in housekeeper, each of whom had their own suites overlooking the pool house. Cleo came from an effortless world.

Not long ago he'd asked Cleo about being rich and she quickly dismissed it. "Oh, we're not *rich* rich. I know lots of people who have way more money than we do. Anyway, money's not that important," she said.

It is to me, thought Alex as he looked around his yard. The trampoline was broken from when one of the twins had jumped onto it from the roof. The umbrella she'd been holding at the time hadn't slowed her down any. The speedboat cover was half off, and the boat was littered with leaves and streaked with mold. The lawn hadn't been cut before winter had come, so it was yellow and scraggly.

The only neat thing about the Ford house was the barn and the field. Turnip was, as always, perfectly turned out, and so was Detroit.

Still, there were a thousand reasons money was important. Alex hated being at the mercy of Ms. Reed and he hated that he was basically a charity case at Limestone. He worked, cleaning stalls and mending fences and maintaining the rings, to pay for his lessons, but even so, Fergus and Ivan were giving him a good deal.

Then there was the issue of gear. He took excellent care of everything he had, but there was so little of it. Cleo's tack and clothes were not only top of the line, they were the best money could buy. And she was so *careless* about all of it. She was always getting in trouble for riding with dirty boots or leaving bridles in a heap, the bits crusted with slobber, or doing a so-so job of grooming her horse. It was like a science with her, or an art: how to get by with the least possible work.

Alex looked at his watch. Cleo still hadn't finished saying good-bye. It was always like this. He practically had to tear her away from Grace and the girls. For some reason Cleo loved hanging around his house. She came over every chance she got and followed Grace and the twins around like a puppy. She loved talking to Grace about her hair and the twins about their desire to become movie stunt women. Didn't she realize how completely screwed up his family was? His father lived in a *motor home* in the front yard, for God's sake.

The smallest, bitterest part of Alex thought Cleo should be satisfied with all her money and leave him the few things that were actually his, like his tacky, unkempt family.

Then he felt bad again for being selfish.

Alex had never had a close friend before. If this was what it felt like, he could do without.

He was just about to go and drag Cleo from the house when he saw Colette Reed's car pull into the driveway.

Great, he thought. *Just what I need*. He lived in constant fear that Ms. Reed was going to change her mind about letting him keep Detroit at home, or worse, take him back entirely. Or what if she asked him to pay some huge leasing fee, which she'd be within her rights to do. Alex's solution was to avoid her as much as possible. An added bonus was that he got to avoid his father at the same time.

Please don't come over here, he thought as he peered cautiously into his rearview mirror at Ms. Reed's car. He heard the front door of the house open and slam shut and saw Cleo stride out. She waved at him but instead of heading for the IROC, she walked over to Ms. Reed's car. He saw her exchange words with his father and Ms. Reed, and then she came trotting back.

"Ready?" she asked, after getting in and slamming the car door.

"Easy on the door," he said. "What were you doing?"

"I was just helping May bandage a fake wound. Maggie's sprained wrist was making it hard for her to help."

"No, I mean what were you talking about with my dad and Ms. Reed?"

"Oh, just now? I was telling them about the clinic. I thought they'd like to come and watch you ride, and I knew *you* wouldn't tell them."

"You did what?"

"I invited them to watch the clinic with the guy from Spain. Your dad should see how well you're doing. He still doesn't understand dressage. This will help. And Colette, if she has half a brain, which I doubt, will be impressed when she sees how you're doing on Detroit."

"The Spanish Riding School is in Vienna," he said in a tight voice. "Which is in Austria. Not Spain."

He hoped she could tell from his voice how angry he was. Unfortunately she wasn't looking at him or listening. She was checking her cell phone for messages.

Alex

ALEX TIGHTENED DETROIT'S girth one more hole. He imagined the instructor asking him to ride a ten-meter circle and him sliding off to the side and then underneath the horse. *Your seat*, the instructor would say, his accent refined and reflective of the Spanish Riding School, *could use some work*. The crowd would laugh, appreciating the joke.

Alex looked down the row of stalls to see if Cleo was getting Tandava ready yet. She wasn't. The mare needed a long, careful warm-up to burn off energy so she was able to focus on her work. But Cleo never took the time to do it. *Too selfish*, Alex thought, and then felt guilty. He'd almost forgiven her for inviting his father and Ms. Reed to this clinic because he'd finally convinced himself that they'd never show up. They were probably loaded when Cleo had told them about it and had forgotten. He could only hope.

He checked his watch and realized he had only twenty minutes to warm Detroit up before his lesson with the Spanish Riding School guy. He pulled on his gloves, which he noticed with dissatisfaction were not leather, straightened his helmet, and led Detroit to the outdoor ring.

The instructor may have attended the Spanish Riding School in Vienna, but he looked straight from the Elderly European Gentleman's Academy of Questionable Taste. The man was old. Older even than Ivan and Fergus. He wore a white turtleneck and a yellow, ankle-length winter coat. He'd gelled his hair back against his head so fiercely it looked as though he'd just gotten out of the pool. He was deeply tanned and had a cigarette lodged in the corner of his mouth. The expression on his face could be summed up as unimpressed.

Alex entered the ring a few minutes before the previous rider finished. The girl was on a lovely gray horse. From the little bit Alex had seen she wasn't a bad rider. She wasn't amazing or anything, but looked as though she had a decent seat and soft hands.

The instructor did not agree.

The man stared at the girl, whose face was red with the effort of riding or maybe the stress of riding in front of the small crowd. The instructor's small black eyes squinted against the smoke that leaked up from his cigarette. The girl kept looking over at him, as though she wasn't sure whether the lesson was over or not.

She slowed her horse to a walk and gave him a furtive pat.

"That was Phillipa Grant on Hernando's Hideaway," the announcer said into her portable microphone. She, too, was looking around like she didn't quite know whether the lesson was over or not.

"Do you have any final comments?" the announcer asked the instructor. The man very slowly took the cigarette from his mouth and spoke loud enough for the microphone to pick up his voice.

"She too fat," he said.

Alex nearly fell off his horse. Every head in the place jerked around. The rider, who was slightly plump but certainly not fat, gaped openmouthed at the instructor like he'd just sprouted horns and a tail.

The announcer tried to smooth things over. "It's winter. Maybe Hernando has been getting too much hay," she said with a weak laugh.

The instructor waved his cigarette around, nearly getting the announcer in the eye. "No," he said. "I mean the rider. She flabby."

"Holy shit," muttered Alex to himself as he wondered what he'd gotten himself into.

The crowd murmured nervously.

The girl on the gray horse was nearly purple now—her face was a mask of anger and hurt feelings. As she rode past Alex he could see that she was blinking back tears.

The announcer lady forged ahead. "Yes, well, ahem. Next up we have Alex Ford riding Detroit. Detroit is a nine-year-old Dutch Warmblood." She cleared her throat nervously and stepped quickly away from the instructor just in case he came at her again with his cigarette.

The man rolled his head on his shoulders as though about to perform a complicated exercise routine, but he said nothing. Alex felt his body stiffen and his heart rate jump. He didn't know what to do. He was used to following directions in lessons, not doing his own thing. Detroit's stride shortened as he picked up on Alex's nerves. From the expression on his face, the instructor might as well have been watching a three-legged goat limp its way around the dressage arena.

Alex rode past the spectators. Fergus leaned forward from his place in the front row of the bleachers and whispered, "Just ride."

Alex nodded. *Pretend you're alone and that this weird little man in the long yellow coat isn't staring at you, getting ready to tell you you're homely or your legs are too skinny or your ears stick out.* He pushed Detroit into a trot. He was still getting used to Detroit's big trot after so many years of riding Turnip's gentle jog. He reminded himself to relax and try to follow the horse's movement. Just as he was finding his rhythm, he heard a commotion near the entryway. A flash of red caught his attention. Someone was signaling him. Alex slowed Detroit to a walk and looked, confused, toward the noise.

"Helloooo!" cried Colette Reed in a loud, inebriated voice. Alex closed his eyes for a moment. This was a nightmare. The only thing that would make it worse was if his dad was here, too. Sure enough, his father stood right behind the redheaded realtor. Even from the other side of the ring Alex could see that his dad's dress shirt was buttoned up wrong and he seemed to be swaying in a nonexistent breeze.

"Bloody Cleo," Alex whispered under his breath. Why couldn't she keep her mouth shut? This was all her fault. Didn't she understand the critical importance of keeping the different parts of one's life separate? This was a dressage clinic, not a beer garden. His father and Ms. Reed had no business being here.

Why couldn't Cleo have kept her mouth shut? As he rode past Ms. Reed and his father he smiled tightly, then looked over at his coaches. Ivan nodded and Alex was reminded of what he'd said about Alex's ability to make the horses believe in themselves. Detroit needed him to keep it together. Besides, it wasn't possible to die of embarrassment or Alex would have been dead a long time ago.

Alex moved Detroit into a trot, sat still for a few beats, and pushed the big horse into a canter. Soon he forgot all about the audience, including the man in the middle of the ring, his father, and his father's girlfriend.

After a few minutes, the man's cigarette came out of his mouth and he took two steps toward Alex, who was circling Detroit on the far side of the ring.

"Yes, yes," he said. "I want to see a bit more straightness."

Don't we all? said the voice in Alex's head, but he just nodded.

"Down the long side, shoulder-in," said the man, puffing vigorously between words.

The yellow-coated man had Alex ride a leg yield across the diagonal, first one way, then the other. He asked for a lengthened stride down the long side at a canter and at a trot. Alex was working so hard, he forgot to worry. By the end of the lesson Detroit had grown lighter in his hand and was swinging through his back. It was a marvelous feeling. Dressage had done it again: blocked out all his troubles.

"This is enough," said the man as he lit another cigarette. "Your horse is a bit out of shape, no?"

Alex nodded.

"He's a nice horse, though. It's perhaps possible do some things with this horse. And you, you have a lot to learn, but it might be possible to do some things with you, also. A bit of natural talent there, I think."

Alex's eyes widened and he swallowed.

The announcer was on her way into the ring when Ms. Reed grabbed her arm.

"That's my horse," said Ms. Reed into the microphone. Then she turned to the small crowd and continued in a theatrically loud voice, "Oh, Brian, isn't it lovely to see your son on *my* horse?"

Alex didn't hear his father's reply. Instead, he quietly thanked the instructor and dismounted. On his way out of the ring he passed Cleo, who was leading Tandava in.

"Well?" she asked, her eyes wide.

He pretended he hadn't heard her and kept walking.

"There you are!" said Ms. Reed, making an unsteady beeline for Alex, dragging Mr. Ford behind her.

"Wasn't he a good boy!" she exclaimed in a high falsetto. She went to touch Detroit and he flinched away from her hand.

"Whoa," whispered Alex.

"I was just speaking to a woman who was saying Detroit would be the perfect horse for her daughter, but I told her that he already has a rider. Can't let my beau's son go without a horse, can I?" she said, staring at Mr. Ford. Alex couldn't read his father's face as he looked at his girlfriend. It wasn't a look of love, that much was definite, and Alex felt a flare of anxiety go through his stomach.

Cleo

WHENEVER YOU GO to a clinic with someone you don't know, you've got a fifty-fifty chance that you'll be dealing with a jerkweed. I knew as soon as I saw Phillipa's face that this guy was from the dark side. Phil should know that when you get a bad one, all you can do is suck it up. She's got Svetlana the Sour Soviet for a coach, for God's sake. You'd think she'd be used to it.

I didn't say that, though. I tried to be sympathetic.

"Hey, Phil, a little rough in there?" I said as I walked past the Stoneleigh trailer where Phil was brushing Hernando. Phil lifted her arms slowly, as though they were made of lead, and every stroke of the brush pushed her closer to the edge of exhaustion.

She didn't turn around even though I knew she heard me.

"Did the guy give you a hard time?" I asked.

This time she did turn around and I saw that her face was blotchy from crying and her lips were kind of white. She looked terrible, to be honest. Not at all attractive.

"He called me fat," she said.

"Oh, shit," I said. Then I caught myself. "You're not fat. You're Rubenesque, or whatever they call that."

Phillipa frowned. "Do you have any idea how much bigger girls hate it when skinny girls try to make them feel better by calling them Rubenesque?"

"Okay, stacked. You're stacked. Is that better?"

This time she did smile a bit.

"Anyway, you definitely aren't fat. The guy's just a nasty old bastard. He's jealous of your youth."

Phil nodded, wiping at her nose with the underside of her wrist in a gesture that was somewhere between ladylike and hayseed-goes-to-town.

"Did you see his hair?" she sniffed.

"Dude, I saw his turtleneck and his yellow coat. That was enough."

"And the way he chain-smokes?"

"Totally. He may not even make it to the end of the clinic. He may just keel over from lung disease in the next hour or so."

She nodded and gave me another weak smile.

"What are you doing later?" she asked.

"Besides licking my wounds after this guy beats me down? I was actually planning to go to Alex's."

"Oh, right," she said. "What about tomorrow? You want to hang out?"

"Actually, I was going to be at the barn and then maybe go by Alex's place again. You know, after."

I should have asked her to join me. I hadn't spent time with her for ages. But I didn't want anyone else coming to Alex's. There barely even seems to be room for me there. So I didn't invite her and Phil's face shuttered again. She nodded, muttered, "Good luck," and went back to brushing her horse.

When I got into the ring, I quickly looked at the instructor. His yellow coat was too big on him and his cheekbones looked carved from stone. He didn't say anything to me, so I walked Tandy. I really wasn't all that nervous because I didn't care what he thought. I'm not like Alex—riding isn't my whole life.

I kept walking Tandy around while I waited for the hatchet-faced man to say something, but he just kept puffing away on his gasper and staring at me like I was a germ he didn't want to catch. I passed Fergus and Ivan, and Fergus whispered, "Ride."

I turned and mouthed, "I am," back at him.

The lesson went on like that for about ten minutes. I just walked Tandy around the ring and the instructor smoked harder and harder.

Usually in a clinic situation, the instructor will ask you to put your horse through its paces so he or she can evaluate what areas you need to work on. Then he or she will ask you to do a few exercises. But this guy wanted to play games. Too bad for him. If he wanted to teach me, he'd better get teaching.

I started gazing up at the roof of the arena to let him know that I wasn't very impressed. That got a reaction: I heard the sharp, irritated intake of breath. When Tandy and I came around the end of the arena again Fergus stood and leaned over the railing. "Stop messing around," he hissed.

Fine. I put Tandy into a trot, then a canter, then brought her right back to a walk. Our transitions were perfect. Take that, Yellow Jacket!

During my time at Limestone, Ivan had ridden

Tandava and practiced her piaffe and passage. He said it was to keep her training up until someday I was ready to ask for those movements.

This lesson was so pointless I decided that it would be sort of fun to blow Herr Hatchet Face's mind by showing him that Tandy and I already knew the high-level movements. Or at least *she* did.

To prepare, I collected Tandava's walk and then asked her to do half steps, which is how you start asking for passage. Passage is a fancy diagonal trot that requires the horse to be extremely collected and to carry a lot of its weight on its haunches. It's an upper-level movement, and I wasn't trained to do it, so I'd never asked for it before. But it was time for me to stop acting like such a sheep and waiting for someone to give me permission. It was time I started pushing the boundaries. I shortened the reins and increased the pressure of my legs. Tandy began to snort softly and she gave me a few half steps. I got this excellent, floaty feeling in my stomach.

What the hell. Might as well go all the way. I tightened my grip on the reins some more, sat back a little, and spurred Tandava on without letting her go forward. She seemed to rise under. She was going to passage! I'd done it!

But she didn't passage. She went up, up, up, hunching her back beneath me. Then she kicked out a back leg. It sounded like a gunshot against the wall of the arena. I wasn't going to let her make a fool of me. I tightened up the reins even more and put the spurs on again.

In response, Tandava leaped into the air, twisting as she went. I dropped one of my reins and she ripped the other one out of my hand as she landed. She reared and I grabbed her mane to hold on. She dropped back onto all fours and tore off bucking across the arena, just barely missing Yellow Jacket. He stepped back like a matador, using his cigarette to wave her through. I held on for the first two bucks, but on the third I lost a stirrup and on the fourth she launched me into the air. I landed on my back and found myself looking up at the arena's roof. I could barely breathe. It felt like both my lungs had collapsed.

The instructor guy walked over and caught Tandy. I know because I saw his boots go by. No one came over to see if I was okay.

I struggled to sit up and when I did, I saw the instructor take off his coat and hand it to Fergus, who'd stepped into the ring. Fergus didn't look at me.

He just held Tandy's reins and patted her neck. The instructor ran his hands down each of Tandy's legs to make sure she wasn't injured.

Next thing I know the instructor, wearing a sweater over a button-down shirt, was on my horse. He patted her and made calming noises. Meanwhile, I was sitting on the ground. I could have been dead, for all anyone seemed to care.

I got up and brushed some of the wood chips and sand off my breeches and I was about to head over to tell the guy to get off my horse, but Fergus held up the Hand of Silence, so all I could do was stand next to him, humiliated. He even gave me the guy's coat to hold, which added insult to injury. We stood there watching while the instructor walked Tandava, trotted her, cantered her, and then asked her to passage. He didn't seem to move his hands or his legs. He was perfectly still. And she passaged and then piaffed like it was her favorite thing in the world. Everyone in the small crowd clapped.

Sometimes I really hate dressage.

After the lesson, I led Tandava out of the ring. Not one person spoke to me, unless you count the instructor guy muttering "useless" under his breath as he handed me my horse. People in the jumping world are fairly matter-of-fact about falls, I guess because they fall quite a lot. People who ride dressage are usually more sympathetic. Unless they're dealing with me.

After my lesson all Fergus did was shake his head at me. The other riders and spectators stared with big eyes, and as soon as I passed them the whispers started.

"Did you see her spur that horse?"

"What was she thinking, trying to passage?"

"She deserved it."

You'd think I'd put an electrode up her ass instead of asked her to do something that she's *supposedly* trained to do.

I said as much to Alex when I got to the Limestone Farm trailer.

"You don't know how to passage," he said.

"I've seen Ivan do it."

"Yeah, and I've heard Mariah Carey hit the high notes, but that doesn't help when I try."

What was his problem? "Why did you ignore me earlier?" I asked, remembering how he blew me off when I was heading into the ring.

"I don't know what you're talking about," he said.

I made a "whatever" noise, but my feelings were hurt. Alex was supposed to be on my side.

"You're really being a jerk," I muttered.

Alex turned to me, brush in hand.

"Then maybe you should think before you act. Think before you speak. Stop acting like a spoiled kid. Then people won't act like jerks."

I was so shocked I just stood there with my mouth open.

"Look, I'm sorry," he said. "I just . . . never mind. I'm sorry you fell off."

"Fine," I sniffed. But it wasn't fine. It wasn't fine at all. I haven't felt that betrayed since, well, Chad. Why do I always seem to pick the wrong people to trust?

"I just need some time on my own," he said.

"Fine," I said again. What else was there to say? It was like he was dumping me but he couldn't dump me since we weren't really together. I felt almost like I'd just fallen again, and had the wind knocked out of me and no one was coming over to see if I was okay.

So, when I got home and Jenny asked if I wanted to go with her to a party, I said yes.

Cleo

JENNY SAYS IT'S a miracle that I hadn't taken up partying earlier. She can barely believe I grew up in L.A. I told her I went to an all-girl private school with a conservative dress code and an emphasis on academics. She said she would have guessed that I went to a private nunnery just north of Neverland.

Since I started hanging out with Jenny a couple of months ago, I've finally begun to experience life. I am such a late bloomer, I can barely believe myself sometimes! I mean, I'm ahead of other people on TV knowledge and getting taken advantage of by certain guys named Chad and getting banished from my home nation as a result, but when it comes to drinking and having fun, I'm practically an infant. Jenny's helping me to fix all that, though.

At that first party I went to with Jenny, back in December, I got drunk for the first time *and* I met a guy! Hello, red-letter day!

The boy, whose name I didn't quite catch because I was a bit drunk, was a superfox. He was so cute he could have been from home. He had killer black hair and freckles across his nose and blue eyes with little flecks of white in them. Ten minutes after we met we ended up kissing in a stairwell. It was fantastic. It may have been the best time I've ever had in my life.

I was still high from the experience (and the clouds of secondhand pot smoke) when I went home for the holidays. Even the crappy twenty-four hours spent with my parents, being reminded about my poor judgment every sixty seconds, and the crappy week that followed, spent with Consuela, whom my parents paid time and a half to act as my chaperone over the holidays, couldn't dampen my excitement to get back to school and Jenny so we could go to another party and see the boy again.

After the clinic with Herr Humorless, I promised Fergus and Ivan that when I got back from California I'd start attacking my chores like I cared and riding for all I was worth during lessons and so on, but I just haven't been able to do it. For one thing, since I got back a month ago, I've been going out with Jenny at least twice a week and it takes me at least two days to feel normal again after one of our "expeditions," as she calls them. On top of that I have school, which is nowhere near as demanding as Marlborough, but they do sort of expect me to attend classes.

Riding is starting to feel like it's interfering with my life or at least the part of my life that could lead to seeing the black-haired boy again. Fergus and Ivan have mentioned about twenty times that the spring show is coming up next month, and I can't make another spectacle of myself. The spring show includes show jumping, hunter, and dressage, so Jenny should be getting ready, too, but she's not. Getting ready isn't her thing.

She almost never goes to class and misses at least half her riding lessons and even quite a few shows. She's had two conferences with Ms. Green about "pulling up her boots" and several strong talking-tos from her jumping coach, but she doesn't seem fazed.

"Aren't you worried about getting kicked out?" I asked her after she got back from yet another disciplinary meeting.

"Nah. They aren't going to kick me out. I'm the best rider they've got." It was true. Jenny might not be very consistent with her training, but when she does get on her horse, they are unstoppable. I've seen Jenny's mare, a Selle Francais named Rio, make it over jumps with Jenny nearly passed out on her back. If Jenny tried even a little bit she could totally make Young Riders. But Jenny's not a trier. There's something kind of refreshing about that.

As we talked, she lay in bed, fully dressed, but with her quilt pulled up to just under her nose. It was four o'clock in the afternoon and she hadn't ridden her horse for at least a week.

"But what if they do?" I couldn't believe she could be so nonchalant.

She closed her eyes. "Don't worry. I won't get kicked out. You won't get kicked out. They expect us to get into trouble. They'd be disappointed if we didn't. I'm going to take a short nap now, but be ready to head out tonight at around nine."

This morning, Fergus was in the indoor ring when I arrived.

"Oooooh! Hiiiiii," he said, *very* sarcastic.

"Hi," I whispered. Speaking too loudly made my

head hurt worse. Jenny and I worked on the doing-shooters part of my education last night.

"Well, it's just been such a delight waiting for you," he said. "You'll notice Ivan isn't here. He left after ten minutes."

"I'm not *that* late."

"Miss Cleo, you are twenty minutes late for a forty-five-minute lesson. And I know for a fact that you only arrived fifteen minutes ago because on my way out to the barn to give you hell, I passed Mrs. Mudd as she was leaving. She gave me a terrible look."

"She's a . . . " I let my voice trail off before completing that thought.

"A fine and patient woman who must be sorely tried having to deal with the likes of you," said Fergus.

"So is my lesson canceled?" I asked, trying not to sound as hopeful as I felt.

He ignored me.

"In this life, we only get so many chances. Some of us squander our chances. Others make the most of them. Which type are you?"

I wished I was the type who was still in bed, but I was smart enough to keep my mouth shut.

"You are riding today—with me. And I plan to be every bit as fierce as Ivan. You've been an absolute twit since you returned from Los Angeles. I don't know what that town did to you, but we've got to get you straightened out before the spring show."

"Oh, that."

"Yes, that. You need to get used to riding in public without making a scene. Competitive dressage riders compete."

"I'm not competitive," I grumbled, leading Tandy over to the mounting block.

"Quite right. You certainly aren't. That's why you are going to spend the next forty-five minutes riding your tail off, and when we're done in here, you and I are going to have a conference with your young colleague, Alex. I understand that you both plan to ride a freestyle. That means you only have a few weeks to prepare your music and your choreography."

"I don't feel ready to ride a freestyle."

"A month ago you insisted that the freestyle was your favorite event. If I recall, you implied you'd *die* if you weren't allowed to ride a freestyle. Well, I'm here to assure you that that's correct. You *will* die if you don't do the work to prepare and to ride one."

"God," I muttered.

"Yes?" said Fergus.

Then the ride began.

Alex

ALEX COULDN'T SEEM to stop working. Sometimes he wondered whether he had a disease of the nervous system. Lately he'd been even more of a maniac for chores than usual. He went to school full time, worked at the barn, looked after two horses, and trained dressage. Cleo kept asking him if he was on drugs. This afternoon it was even getting on Fergus's nerves.

"Lad, please. I'm trying to nag here and you're making me feel superfluous," said Fergus.

"Sorry," said Alex as he put down one of Tandava's leg wraps he was untangling.

"As I was saying," Fergus began again. "You both plan to ride a freestyle in the schooling show next month. You two will be representing this fine establishment and we don't want you embarrassing us by riding some terrible tests set to dreadful music. So how are they coming?"

"I did my choreography," said Alex quietly.

"That's wonderful. Have you picked your music?"

Alex shook his head.

Fergus leaned against the doorway of the tack room where Alex worked while Cleo watched.

"We've timed your horses with the metronome. Now you both need to pick music. And Miss Cleo has to design her choreography, since she has done nothing."

Fergus pointed at Alex. "Ride home safely. I'm still not comfortable with this wagon-train arrangement of yours."

"It's okay," said Alex.

He knew his coach got a kick out of the way Alex rode Turnip and led Detroit behind, like the world's biggest pack pony. The routine kept Turnip feeling useful and as long as the old paint led the way, Detroit was happy to follow.

After Fergus left, Alex extracted another polo wrap from the large tangled pile at his feet.

"Sorry," Cleo said. "I guess I shouldn't wash so many at once."

"Don't worry about it."

Things between Alex and Cleo had been strained ever since their argument at the clinic. It didn't help that Cleo seemed to have gone wild over the holidays. Instead of hanging around his place, she went out with her roommate several nights each week. He was surprised to find that he missed her and her constant questions and advice, and he worried about her drastic change in lifestyle. It was like watching Mary Poppins get mixed up with the wrong crowd.

"You want to go look for music for your freestyle?" Cleo asked.

"I might have something I can use at home."

"Please, I've seen your music collection and it sucks. You've got like four CDs and they were all gift with purchase. You can't ride a good freestyle to soft jazz hits. The judges might be old, but that doesn't mean they'll be deaf. You need to find something exciting. We'll go to the record store and listen to different stuff to get ideas."

Alex sighed, pulled another polo wrap free of the pile, and began to roll it, inside out, on top of his knee. There was no use arguing with her once she got an idea. And he didn't completely hate the idea of spending time with Cleo. He was just about to say yes, when she spoke up again.

"Tell you what. Mrs. Mudd has been complaining about driving me back and forth from school every day, so my parents said I could get a car. We can go music *and* car shopping this weekend."

Alex shot Cleo a sideways glance. *Car shopping?* This he had to see.

"Okay," he said.

"Awesome. So you'll pick me up Saturday morning?"

Alex nodded.

"We are going to have such a good time. Hey, I'm going out with Jenny Thursday night. You want to come?"

Alex shook his head. "No. I better not. I've got stuff to do," he said.

Cleo got up to leave when she heard the rumble of Mrs. Mudd's truck outside.

"Later skater," she said.

He nodded and looked back down. He was still up to his knees in tangled polos.

Alex

IT TOOK ALEX only a few minutes to realize that Cleo was a major-league shopper.

The first thing she said to him when she got into the IROC Saturday morning was, "Where are the import dealerships in this town?"

Alex didn't know. But he didn't want to admit that, since he was a guy and his father owned a used RV dealership on the outskirts of town. He felt like it was his job to know exactly where all of the car and tractor places were. After all, car dealerships lined most of the major streets in Nanaimo, their glass-sided buildings marooned in a sea of new cars, flags flying, sun glinting off the windshields.

"I think there's one on Bowen Road. Somewhere

around there, anyway."

"Excellent," she said.

"So you're just going to buy a car? Like today?"

Cleo looked at him and frowned slightly. "Yeah."

"Oh. Are you going riding after?"

She had on a pair of suede breeches under brown leather riding boots and a short shearling jacket.

"Nah," she said. Then she noticed him looking at her outfit. "I don't want them to think I'm some nobody. You can't drive up to a car dealership in an IROC and expect to be treated seriously."

"But if you look like you're going horseback riding, everything will be fine?"

"Yeah."

"What about the whole getting-gouged thing? You know, if they think you have money."

"I do have money," she said fondly, as though she was speaking to a learning-disabled child. "The point is to have a nice shopping experience. We're teenagers and they aren't going to let us test-drive nice cars if they think we're poor."

"Right," he said, glancing down at his outfit of heavy wool plaid coat, cords, boots, and a knitted cap. He briefly imagined changing into his show clothes, the two of them arriving at the European car dealership looking like they'd just stepped off the pages of *Vanity Fair*. He imagined bringing along a pair of trusty hunting dogs to complete the picture. He sort of liked the image. Oh well, it was too late to get changed. Cleo would just have to pretend she was shopping with her gardener.

He drove the IROC along the main roads while Cleo looked for dealership signs.

"Ford. Keep going!"

Alex was a bit insulted until he realized she was referring to the dealership.

"Cadillac! Maybe we should stop. It would be so old school to drive a Caddy."

Her words came too late. He'd already driven past the turnoff. They drove along a stretch of highway lined with malls and car dealerships.

"Think you have enough freakin' malls in this town?" Cleo asked, as though Alex had personally financed and built them all.

"You're the one going shopping," he pointed out.

"Yeah, but I don't want to *feel* like I'm shopping. I want to feel like I'm just going for a little walk, cruising cafés and art galleries, gathering culture and worldly knowledge and I just happened to come upon this amazing little car store, tucked among the trees, birds twittering overhead."

"Didn't Americans invent the strip mall?" he asked.

"Don't play the blame game," she said. "It's so unattractive."

When they reached Rutherford Road, Cleo looked over and saw the VW dealership sign.

"Cool! V-Dub!" she exclaimed.

"I'm in the wrong lane."

"So turn right and then do a U-ey."

Alex frowned at her. There would be no U-eys while he was driving. He turned right, then left, and left again, landing them in a McDonald's parking lot. They ended up trapped in the lineup for the drive-through lane.

"May I take your order?" asked the crackly voice emanating from the speaker.

"Nothing," said Alex.

"I'm sorry," said the voice. "I didn't hear that."

Cleo leaned over Alex and shouted, *"Nothing! We're in the wrong lane. Because he refuses to do U-eys!"*

"I'm sorry," said the voice. "I didn't hear that. May I take your order?"

After they escaped the McDonald's with a small

order of fries, Alex experienced a few tense moments trying to pull into the VW dealership.

"Left! Left!" shrieked Cleo. "You're going to miss it! We're going to end up back in McDonald's."

"The turnoff is a one-way," said Alex through gritted teeth. "Going the *other* way."

This trip was turning into Alex's worst nightmare. It was bad enough when his sisters and aunt and Cleo teased him about his lack of driving skills. The thought of a group of potentially attractive mechanics seeing him in action was almost too much.

He slowed the IROC to a crawl and drove behind a row of garages and oil-change places. The car rumbled embarrassingly. He prayed it wouldn't stall.

"Pull in there," said Cleo, pointing to an empty spot between a row of plastic-wrapped VW Bugs.

She was out of the car before he stopped the engine. He grabbed the fries so he'd have something to hold on to and followed her.

Four salesmen stood at the door of the sales center. They looked at the IROC, at Alex and Cleo, and three of them turned away.

"Hello," said the remaining salesman. Alex had seen enough episodes of *What Not to Wear* to know that the guy's suit didn't fit very well. The sleeves looked too short and there were strange puckers in the fabric around the arms.

He was young, too, more of a salesboy than a salesman. Alex had expected someone more like his dad's RV sales guys: older, with a paunch and lots of unfortunate jewelry. He hadn't expected a guy who looked like he was just out of high school and wearing his first suit.

The boy extended his hand toward Alex, who quickly stepped back and pointed at Cleo.

"Her. She's looking for a car. I'm just, uh . . ." He looked down at the container of French fries in his hand. "Eating fries."

The guy shook Cleo's hand and seemed to notice her outfit for the first time.

"You look like . . ." His voice trailed off as he struggled for words to describe this look that he recognized but couldn't quite name.

"I attend an *equestrienne* school," said Cleo.

Alex squinted at her. Was she using some kind of accent?

"Oh," said the salesboy. His hair was combed back and still damp. Alex felt a rush of sympathy.

"I'm in the market for a vehicle," Cleo announced.

The salesboy blushed deeply. "Are your, uh, parents coming?"

"I'm nearly seventeen," said Cleo, her voice now offended as well as self-important.

Alex ate a fry.

"I'll be putting the deposit on my credit card. My mom will send the rest."

"Oh," said the salesboy.

The fry stopped halfway down Alex's throat.

"So you're interested in a Golf or maybe a Bug?"

Cleo wrinkled her nose and put her hands on her slim hips. "Noooo. I don't think so."

She looked around and then pointed at a large, shiny station wagon with elaborate hubcaps.

"What's that?"

"That's the Passat Wagon."

"That looks nice."

Alex's French fry was stuck somewhere in the vicinity of his esophagus.

"It's kind of an expensive car," said the salesboy uncertainly.

Cleo ignored him and spoke to Alex. "I don't want to be some cliché boarding-school girl, you know, driving around in a Beemer or whatever. That car looks mature. Dignified. It looks like a dressage car."

In Alex's mind a dressage ride was a truck that could pull a horse trailer, but he wasn't about to argue.

The salesboy took a deep breath and started his spiel as though reading it straight out of the sales manual.

"The Passat Wagon is very popular with customers who care about safety and comfort. It's ideal for people with small children. You've got your two-liter, two hundred horsepower, six-speed manual all the way to your three-point-six-liter V6R with two hundred eighty horsepower, six-speed automatic with Triptronic."

Cleo pursed her lips. "You know," she said. "I don't really care."

"Oh," said the boy.

Alex resisted the urge to offer him a fry.

"I do like the sounds of that Trip stuff, but mainly what I'm after is a big, shiny new car."

"It's forty-seven thousand dollars before tax or extras," whispered the salesboy.

"Perfect," said Cleo. She reached into her purse and handed him her credit card. "I think there's like twenty on there. My mom will send you the rest."

"Don't you want to take it for a test-drive?" said

the boy in a strangled voice.

"I suppose." Cleo's tone made it clear that she couldn't care less.

The salesboy looked at Alex, who shrugged and ate another fry.

After the boy went in to get the dealer plates and run Cleo's credit card, he came back accompanied by an older man wearing a much better suit. He was one of the men who'd turned away when Alex and Cleo had first pulled up.

"Well, hey there," he said. "I'm Peter. I'm the manager here. Sam tells me you're interested in putting a deposit on the Passat Wagon."

Cleo looked bored.

"Do you have another piece of ID, honey?"

Cleo sighed and dug around in her purse and pulled out her passport and her driver's license. The man checked it against her credit card.

"Well," he said, suddenly much friendlier. "Feel free to ask me any questions Sam hasn't been able to answer."

"Actually, Sam doesn't need any help," said Cleo. "He just sold me what I assume is the most expensive car on the lot." She looked down at her watch. "In five minutes. Sam is quite a salesman."

Alex and Sam looked at each other, then Alex smiled down at his French fries. Cleo could be a pain sometimes, but she definitely had style.

After the manager went back inside, Sam attached the dealer plates and helped Cleo into the car.

"You coming?" Cleo asked Alex, who stood to the side with the now-empty French fry container in his hand.

"I'll wait here."

Cleo's behavior as a passenger made him suspect that she might not be a very good driver.

"Oh, shut up, you're coming."

Sam, the salesboy, opened the backseat and Alex got in. He was immediately enveloped by the smell of leather and new car.

The moment Sam closed his door, Cleo threw the car into reverse.

"Whoa," said Sam. "I guess you're pretty excited."

From his vantage point in the back of the car, Alex could see that Cleo was hunched over the steering wheel. There was something about the aggressive tilt of her blond head that made him nervous.

"You'll notice the instrumentation panel is—holy crap!" exploded Sam, as Cleo barely missed clipping a car on her way out of the crowded parking lot.

"I'm sorry. It's just that that was a little close."

After making a series of illegal turns, Cleo got onto the highway. Traffic was heavy and moving slowly. At least, most of it was. The Volkswagen Passat swerved in and out of the fast lane, darting around slower-moving vehicles like a bionic rabbit in a field of three-legged tortoises.

"Hey, Sam, has this thing got air bags?" asked Cleo after an excruciatingly close call with a panel van.

"God, I hope so," said Sam in a small voice. When they finally stopped at a light he said, "Okay, I think you've got a pretty good idea of how it runs. What say we head back to the office now and I'll fill out the paperwork for you?"

"Already?" said Cleo.

"Yes!" shouted Alex from the backseat.

When Cleo screeched to a stop in the dealership lot, Sam practically leaped out of the passenger seat.

Cleo turned back to Alex with one of her eyebrows raised.

"I think that young man earned his commission today."

Alex just nodded as he waited for his heart rate to drop back to its normal range.

After establishing that it would take a few days to get the exact car she wanted and that Sam would deliver it to Stoneleigh for her, Alex and Cleo headed downtown. Cleo hadn't spent much time in downtown Nanaimo and pronounced it "way less divey than I thought!" Alex had to follow her into store after store and watch in awe tinged with horror as she bought everything she laid eyes on.

At the Flying Fish gift shop she purchased a leather ottoman, which Alex calculated cost the same as a custom bridle. She also bought a large wicker wall unit (equivalent to the price of a decent saddle or artificial insemination by a so-so stallion) and a fake zebra-skin carpet (three months' worth of horse-shoeing).

"Don't they give you furniture in your dorm rooms?" he asked when the saleslady was out of earshot.

"Yeah, but I don't love it," said Cleo. "I think this will give us a much better atmosphere for studying."

After she made arrangements to have her new furnishings dropped off at the school and then changed her mind, squealing, "No, wait! I will pick them up next week in my new *station wagon*!", Alex had had enough. She was like a kid on a sugar high.

He propelled her out of the store.

"Okay. We're here to go to the record shop. Now."

"Oh, but there's a cute café over there!" She pointed over his shoulder. "And there's an art gallery right beside it!"

"Music first," he said.

"I was just hitting my stride," she whined.

They walked down the narrow streets, Alex pulling Cleo back every time she tried to go darting into an "adorable bakery!" or "the most awesome little skater shop!"

"Later," he said, reflecting that this must be what it was like to try and shop with a toddler—a toddler with a giant credit limit. It occurred to him that he was no longer irritated with Cleo. He felt sort of fatherly, instead. As he ushered her along, his voice deepened. "Come along now," he said, looking fondly as she skipped up the street in front of him.

When they reached the music store, which was located in an ungainly purple building, he walked boldly up to the door and tugged. It didn't budge.

"They must be closed," he said.

Meanwhile Cleo had found the customer entrance and held the door open for him.

So much for pretending he was the kind of person

who haunts record stores and is up to the minute in his musical tastes.

"I download most of my music," he mumbled as he walked past her and through the real doors. That wasn't true, of course. He was afraid that the first time he downloaded a song, the FBI, CIA, RCMP, and Interpol would swoop down on his house in helicopters. No way was he taking the chance. Plus, he wouldn't have known what to download, since most of the time he listened to whatever radio station was playing in the barn.

The front of the store was filled with televisions and stereos. Alex looked around, unsure where to go.

"Back here," said Cleo. He followed her up a step and into the back of the store.

"So what do you like to listen to?" she asked, waving a hand around the store like she was a majority shareholder.

"I don't know. What are you going to use?"

"I've decided I'm going to buy my freestyle music. There's a woman who'll put it together for you."

"Oh," he said. He'd heard of that woman. She did a great job, but there was no way he could afford to hire her.

Alex stood uncertainly in the back of the store for

a moment, looking at the racks of CDs and DVDs. A clerk in a black T-shirt that read ARCADE FIRE sat at a stool behind the special orders desk. He carefully avoided looking at Alex and Cleo.

"What kind of music does Detroit bring to mind?" Cleo asked.

The big gelding had a relentless curiosity about the world as well as a certain dignity and quiet reserve with strangers. He was a horse who had opinions.

"I don't know. Maybe something kind of . . ." Alex struggled to find the words. He moved his hand to indicate waves.

Cleo squinted. She waved a hand back at him. "What does this mean?"

"To me that means sinewy," said Sofia, coming out from behind a rack. She wore dark-red lipstick and her black hair fell in a sheet to her shoulders. She wasn't wearing her glasses. She looked very beautiful. Alex noticed the music clerk staring at her.

"Can I touch you?" Sofia asked, making a show of reaching for his shoulder. "I want to make sure you're real. I was beginning to think you didn't exist outside of school. And the barn. Hey, Chris!" she called. "Look who's here!" A moment later Chris appeared behind her. When he saw Alex his face broke into a wide smile.

Alex was surprised at how pleased he was to see them.

"What are you guys doing?" he asked.

"If you want to see Chris outside of school, you have to be willing to go to the record stores," said Sofia. "But the real mystery is what you are doing out of the barn."

"We're trying to find some music for Alex's freestyle. That's a dressage test set to music," Cleo replied.

"Cool," said Chris.

"Yeah, the music's supposed to match your horse," she continued. "I was just asking Alex to describe his horse. So far he's come up with . . ." She mimicked him waving his hand.

"Is that the horse we met?" Sofia asked.

"Turnip," said Chris.

Alex felt oddly touched that Chris had remembered his horse's name.

He shook his head. "No. I'm riding a different horse now. Turnip is sort of retired."

"So you need a style of music that suits the horse?" Chris had pushed back his giant headphones so they cupped the sides of his neck.

"The beats in the music are actually supposed to match the footfalls of the front feet at the walk and trot. At the canter, the beats are supposed to match the downbeat of the horse's leading foreleg. We use a metronome to figure out the tempo of each of the different gaits." Alex abruptly fell silent, realizing he sounded like a textbook.

"*Then* you're supposed to consider the horse's style on top of that," added Cleo.

"And so far all you've decided is that your new horse is . . ." Sofia waggled her hand around and grinned.

"No, I've timed him and done the choreography of the test. I just don't know what kind of music to use," said Alex. As he spoke, it suddenly came to him that he was talking to not one, but *three* people. And those three people *were his friends*! The sensation was strange but also thrilling. This, he thought, must be what it's like to be popular. To have a social life.

An image popped into his head of himself wearing a crown. He was surrounded by adoring fans. He stepped onto a stage where he was handed the reins to the world's most beautiful horse. Sitting astride the horse, shirtless, would be . . .

"Alex?" said Cleo, rudely pulling him back to the

present and ending his fantasy. "What kind of music?"

"Well, probably not death metal or gangster rap," he said, and then blushed because he wasn't used to making jokes.

"How would you describe your new horse?" asked Chris, getting into the challenge.

"Well, he's not my horse," Alex said. "But he's kind of athletic and, I don't know, deep."

"He's handsome," said Cleo. "And graceful."

"There's something kind of mysterious about him. Like I could see him running along a tropical beach somewhere after a shipwreck," said Alex. Then he really blushed, because now he was letting on about his Black Stallion fantasies.

"I think I get it," said Chris, nodding seriously.

Cleo squinted at Alex. "My God, are you being *eloquent*?"

Alex shrugged.

"Okay," said Sofia. "We've got athletic, deep, graceful, mysterious, elegant, exotic." She ticked each adjective off on her fingers. "I'm going to make an executive decision and rule out Korn."

"What about bhangra?" asked Chris.

"Isn't that the stuff your aunt listens to?" Cleo asked Alex. He nodded and as soon as he thought of the insistent rhythms of the East Indian dance music he knew Chris was right.

"That could work," he said.

"It's very cool. Very rhythmic," said Chris. Alex noticed that his friend had on a Pixies T-shirt under his old cardigan. He found himself wishing he was familiar with the band so he could say something intelligent about them.

"The world music section's over here," said Sofia, and the four of them walked over to the rack. The India section had about ten CDs in it, and none of them seemed to be bhangra.

"Let's ask the clerk," said Cleo. She led the way to the special orders desk. The clerk peeked up when he saw her coming and quickly looked back down again.

"Excuse me," Cleo said. "Do you have banga music?"

"Bhangra," Chris corrected quietly.

The clerk reluctantly raised his head. "Do we have what?"

He had longish straight black hair, parted in the middle, and a sharp widow's peak. He kept glancing at Sofia.

"Bhangra," said Cleo. "It's an extremely popular type of music."

"It's East Indian dance music, but it's contemporary," added Sofia. "It's got a bit of hip-hop and electronica. Even disco."

The clerk unfolded his long, gaunt body, got off his stool, and walked over to the rack they'd just been looking at.

"The India section's right here," he said. Then he shot another surreptitious glance at Sofia and walked quickly away.

"He was totally checking you out," said Cleo, impressed.

Now it was Sofia's turn to look uncomfortable.

"I've got some bhangra," said Chris. "At home."

"So does his aunt," added Cleo.

"Good. We can listen to a bunch of stuff. See what fits," said Chris.

"Alex is going to need help putting the music together. You know, mixing it so it matches the different movements," continued Cleo.

"Chris can do that!" said Sofia.

Chris nodded.

"You two should make a date," said Cleo. Alex refused to look at Chris. He focused on a large poster for a rock band. The poster described them as THE BIGGEST BAND IN THE WORLD. He'd never heard of them.

"I can come to your place if you want," said Chris.

"He videotaped his test," said Cleo. "You guys can watch that to check for timing."

"Right on." Chris smiled and Alex noticed the sprinkle of freckles across the bridge of his nose. Alex reminded himself that Chris wasn't interested in him. He was probably interested in Cleo. Or Sofia.

"How about Monday after school?" asked Chris.

Alex nodded and then tried to look as non-inappropriately interested as possible. He only barely stopped himself from giving Chris a punch in the arm as he nodded back.

"Super," he said, and immediately regretted it.

"Okay. We've got to book. I'm going to be late for French tutoring this afternoon," said Sofia.

As soon as Chris and Sofia were gone, Cleo turned to Alex. "Just in case you're blind, that guy, who, by the way, is incredibly cute, likes you."

"He's a friend."

"Alex, if you spent any time looking at anything other than horses, you'd see what I mean. I'm telling you he likes you."

"Please," said Alex, but his heart gave a little skip as Cleo's suggestion worked its way into his mind.

"You are a social being. A teenage male who is

capable of having fun. Hey, why don't you come to the party with Jenny and me tonight and I'll prove it to you."

Alex didn't answer.

"Come *on*," said Cleo. "It's time you figured out that there's more to life than just riding."

Alex was as surprised as Cleo when he found himself nodding yes.

19

Alex

"IT'S SATURDAY NIGHT," said Cleo, slurring her words just a bit. "It's not like we're showing tomorrow. We'll stay five more minutes and then we can go. I know he's going to come. I can sense it." Cleo tried to swing her arm affectionately around Alex's neck, but ended up cuffing him in the head.

He couldn't believe he'd let her talk him into driving her and her roommate to this party. The roommate, a big blond girl, disappeared quickly, leaving him and Cleo alone in a crowd of strangers in the basement of this house in Ladysmith. All the fun from their shopping afternoon had disappeared. Now he was just tired and uncomfortable.

"I should get going," he hinted, trying for the

twentieth time to get her to budge.

Cleo leaned onto him from her place on the arm of the threadbare orange love seat. Her elbow poked painfully into his shoulder. They were supposedly waiting for the elusive boy she'd met just before Christmas. So far her relationship with Mr. Right involved making out with him in public at house parties. She wasn't even sure of the boy's name. The guy's friends called him Rob, but she thought that might be his last name.

When Alex was tempted to think of Cleo's personal life as pathetic, he had to remind himself that she was doing better than he was. He was 100 percent romance-free and had resigned himself to staying that way until he was out of high school. Maybe until he was dead.

Alex vaguely recognized a few of the people around them. He thought a couple of them went to his school in Cedar, although he was so far out of the social loop he wasn't even sure. They were mostly druggies and skaters, boys with haircuts that ranged from mod to dirty disco freak circa 1975, girls in low-rise tight jeans with T-shirts cropped short to show their pierced navels. Eminem and 50 Cent were on the stereo, giving him a headache.

"I've got to go," he said. He was stopped by Cleo's death grip on his arm.

"He's here," she said. "Oh my God, look over there. He's here!"

Alex followed her gaze. There, in the entrance to the living room, stood a boy. His black hair was longish, and it fell into his eyes. He held a skateboard tipped up at his side and his loose jeans were held up by a belt with a big silver buckle. The boy's blue eyes locked on Alex's and Alex felt his chest constrict at the same time as Cleo whispered, "It's him! And he's totally looking at me."

As the black-haired boy got closer, Alex felt himself go very still. Cleo slid down beside him onto the couch so she was almost in his lap.

"Hey," said the boy. He smiled but his eyes were appraising.

Cleo grinned, bleary but ecstatic.

"This is my friend Alex," she said, her voice coy.

The boy's smile widened. "Hey, Alex. I'm Cameron."

Alex felt like someone had punched him, if it was possible to be punched in a good way.

Cameron stared at Alex for an extralong few seconds, then turned his attention back to Cleo.

"Alex and I ride together," said Cleo. "We're just friends."

Cameron laughed. "Right on. All I ride is my skateboard."

In the dim light of the party Cameron's blue eyes were cast into shadow. There was a slick confidence and a hunger about him that made Alex's stomach jump.

"Alex does dressage. He's really good," said Cleo.

Cameron nodded, his eyelids hooded and heavy.

"I bet he is," he said. "So you guys want to get high?"

By the time Cameron and Cleo had smoked a joint and Cleo had one more beer it was one o'clock in the morning and Alex was ready to crawl out of his own skin. He'd never been to a party like this before. The clouds of smoke made his throat hurt and the music and people made his head ache. Being so close to Cameron made him want to dive underwater and stay there.

Cleo lay on the couch, her head on Alex's lap, her feet on Cameron's. She was too loaded to talk, but she wasn't quite asleep, either.

"Look, I've got to go. I've got to ride in the morning," said Alex.

"I'll help you take her home."

Alex was relieved. He didn't want to leave Cleo at

the party, but knew she'd protest if he tried to pull her away from Cameron.

"Come on," said Cameron, sliding out from under Cleo's legs. The two boys sat her up, then hoisted her off the couch. They walked her past her roommate, Jenny, who sat beside another girl, on the floor, just inside a darkened hallway.

"Hey," she said. Her eyes were glassy and unblinking.

"We're going to take Cleo home. You want to catch a ride?" Alex asked her.

"No worries," said Jenny as she rocked back and forth to the music.

Cameron and Alex half walked, half dragged Cleo out of the basement, up a short set of concrete stairs, and onto the wet, dark street. Their arms touched where they met behind Cleo's thin back.

"Good thing she's not very big," said Cameron. "She's like a little bird or something."

Cleo stirred between them; she seemed about to speak but then her head dropped back down.

"There's more to her than you might think," said Alex softly.

"Sorry?"

"Oh, nothing. My car's over here."

As they approached the IROC, Cameron laughed.

"Nice ride," he said.

"It's my dad's. Or it was."

They folded Cleo into the backseat and then drove in silence out of Ladysmith back toward Yellow Point. At this hour the streets were quiet and black, except for the odd car full of teenagers spinning through the rain.

Alex was so busy trying not to be aware of the boy beside him, he jumped when Cameron spoke.

"You go to school out here?" he asked as Alex turned onto Yellow Point Road.

"Yeah. Cedar. You?"

"Not really in school right now," said Cameron.

They didn't speak again until Alex pulled the car over to the side of the road outside the entrance to Stoneleigh.

"This way," Alex directed. They carried Cleo along a brick path that led to the back of her dorm. She'd told him enough times how the girls snuck in and out of the school to know where to take her. When they reached the back door, which had been propped open with a stick, Alex and Cameron turned Cleo so she was looking at them.

"Cleo," Alex whispered. "Wake up. You're home."

When Cleo opened her eyes, Alex thought he could see his face reflected in them.

"I love you, Chad," she whispered, and her eyes fell shut again.

Cameron made a face at Alex.

"That makes a guy feel special."

"Cleo," Alex persisted. "Wake up. You have to go in now."

"Okay," she said. Then, like a sleepy child, she walked through the open door and let it shut gently behind her.

Alex and Cameron walked back to the car in silence. When they reached the road Alex turned to Cameron.

"If you tell me where you live, I'll give you a ride home," he said, wondering if Cameron could hear his heart pounding.

"Thanks, buddy," said Cameron, his voice hoarse. "And maybe you should give me your phone number."

Alex couldn't see the other boy very well in the dark but he could sense his body and smell his after-shave and the spicy scent of marijuana, and when Cameron leaned forward and, without speaking a word, kissed him under the flickering streetlight, Alex was only half surprised.

Alex

THE NOTE LAY on the counter when Alex walked into the kitchen the next afternoon.

> *Alex,*
> *Someone named Cameron called. He said*
> *he'll try back later.*
>
> *Maggie*

Ever since the kiss Alex had been veering between feelings of guilt and excitement. He'd almost convinced himself that the previous night was a dream. He never in a million years thought Cameron would call.

He walked quickly from the kitchen to the living

room and back. Unbidden, his friend Chris's face popped into his thoughts. He gave his head a shake and kept walking. He stopped in his tracks—he was filthy. He had to get cleaned up! He raced into the bathroom and began peeling off his clothes. Without waiting for the water to heat up, he jumped into the icy spray of the shower.

From under the hiss of the water he heard something. Was that the phone?

Alex grabbed a towel and raced out of the bathroom, leaving the shower running behind him.

"Where's the phone? Can someone get the phone?" he yelled.

"All right already," came the reply.

May came out of the TV room holding the receiver.

"It's for Grace. A hair appointment."

Alex's heart rate dropped back into normal range.

"Yeesh," said May. "Since when do you care about the phone? You're really starting to worry me."

Alex padded back into the bathroom, suddenly feeling chilled.

Now the water was too hot and it scalded his arm as he reached under the spray to turn it down. He stepped back into the shower and grabbed the shampoo bottle.

Cameron had called. Now what?

He thought of the conversation he'd had with Cleo when she finally dragged herself to the barn at one o'clock that afternoon.

"Well, what did you think of Rob?" she'd asked. "Isn't he gorgeous?"

She didn't even know Cameron's name. How serious could she be about him?

"He seems nice."

"You could tell that we have a connection, right?"

"Sure, I guess."

"Do you think he likes me?"

"I don't know. I'm not good with these things."

"He's got to be into me. We've hooked up three times now."

Actually, Alex felt like correcting her, *you didn't hook up with him last night. I did.* Alex wondered whether Cleo and Cameron had really been together those times she said they had, or had Cleo gotten so trashed she just assumed they had?

"Nothing really happened last night and I'm not blaming you or anything, but if there hadn't been a third party between us . . . well, who knows. And we still sat, thigh-to-burning-thigh, on the love seat. My memory after that is kind of sketchy. All I remember is that you guys took me home and then I threw up. Did he and I, you know, kiss? When you dropped me off?"

"I don't think so."

"Damn," she said. "Next time I'll wear tighter jeans."

Where exactly was he supposed to slip his your-crush-kissed-me confession into that conversation?

Alex wondered if the situation would be any easier if everyone involved was straight; if he and Cameron were friends and they were both after Cleo. Then they could have a fistfight and the winner would ride off into the sunset with the girl. Alex's mind refused to cooperate with that scenario, however. When he tried to imagine it, he and Cameron started out fighting, then fell to the ground in a clinch. *God*, thought Alex, *I can't even* imagine *being straight*. He thought he might be the gayest guy alive.

"Ugh," he said out loud, as he thrust his head back under the stream of hot water.

Alex dried off and went up to his room to change. When he came back downstairs to begin making dinner, he found Colette Reed sitting in the living room. Alone. That meant his sisters and aunt were hiding in their rooms.

"Hi," he said. He worked hard to get a smile onto his face.

Ms. Reed was in a sapphire-blue suit. Her liberally applied perfume made Alex's nose run.

"Alex," she said.

So she was sober. She only remembered his name when she was sober. Alex wondered how Ms. Reed, who was loaded almost every night and all day on weekends, maintained her career. Grace said it was because the people she did business with were just as bad. Alex grudgingly respected that at least she kept herself together enough to run her business during the week. His father didn't even seem able to do that. He hardly even went to the dealership anymore. As far as Alex could tell, one of the senior sales guys was basically running the place.

"How's my horse?" she asked. The question sent a thrill of fear through him. Her horse. There was no getting around the fact that Detroit was her horse. She was always reminding Alex.

"He's good. Are you sure you won't let me pay you to ride him?" he asked, even though he knew she'd say no and that even if she said yes, he had no money to pay her.

"No, that's not necessary. After all, we're practically

family," she said, her red lips in a thin line.

"Yeah. I guess so."

"Your father's not home," she said, and her lips stretched back. Alex thought she looked like one of those brightly colored tropical frogs about to catch a fly.

"Ah, no."

"And he's not at work."

"Really?"

"Really. So I thought I'd wait for him here."

"Oh. Okay. Great. You want to come and see Detroit? I'm just heading out to feed him and Mr. T."

"Not really," she said. But she stood and put on her long fur coat and followed Alex out of the house. She picked her way carefully across the driveway after first casting a long, suspicious look in the direction of the RV.

Alex exhaled a visible breath into the cold evening air and tried to think of something to say. "So," he said. It was the best he could do on short notice.

Ms. Reed ignored him.

Inside the fence, they were immediately joined by both horses. Turnip was first. He trotted over and dropped his head to Alex's chest.

"Hey, old man," said Alex, giving the horse's ears

a scratch. Detroit stood at Turnip's flank and whick-ered his own greeting. "And hello to you, big man."

Alex turned to Ms. Reed. "You'd think they hadn't seen anyone in days. I just saw them an hour ago."

"Mmmm," she said, turning her head toward the RV.

"You go ahead," said Alex. "I don't want them to get you dirty."

Ms. Reed stepped into the barn and he followed her, drawing the heavy rope across the entrance so the horses wouldn't follow them in while he prepared their dinners.

The small barn was as clean as the house was untidy. Alex switched on the light in the tack and feed room.

"I'll be glad when the days start getting longer," he said as he weighed their hay, measured out their pel-lets and supplements, and cut a carrot and an apple into each rubber bucket. He was grateful that at least his dad always paid the horses' feed bills—eventually.

Finally Ms. Reed seemed to notice what he was doing. "You really do fuss around, don't you?"

Alex looked up and adjusted his knitted hat.

"Horses—" he began and then stopped, worried that she might take anything he said as a criticism.

"Horses are for barn girls and boys to take care of," said Ms. Reed. Her head went up like a dog catching a scent on the wind.

A second later, Alex heard the sound of an engine.

"I guess my dad's home," he said, but she was already on her way out the door.

After he'd put the horses in their stalls for the night he headed back into the house. As he passed the RV he saw movement behind the slat blinds and heard raised voices.

Inside the house, he crouched over to take off his boots and was nearly impaled when May stuck the phone under his nose.

"Phone!" she said and took off.

Alex grabbed the receiver.

"Whatcha doing, buddy?" It was Cameron's voice.

"Nothing," he said, and felt a flash of heat burn down his spine.

"You want to do something?"

"Do something?"

"Come down to Bowen Park."

"Tonight?"

"Yeah."

"Now?" Alex tried to keep the confusion and alarm out of his voice. "It's kind of dark."

"Are you scared of the dark?"

"No, I'm just saying."

"Half an hour. I'll meet you in the far lot."

The phone went dead and Alex was left staring down at his untied boots.

The night was dark, but not as dark as he feared, because the moon was nearly full. Alex drove through downtown Nanaimo and up Bowen Road. He turned onto the wet, winding road that led into the park and drove until he reached what he hoped was the farthest lot. He hadn't been to the park since he was little and his class had come to visit the 4-H petting farm. He'd heard a few months back that someone had broken into the little fenced area and beaten several of the baby animals to death. The thought of it made him feel nauseous, as did his knowledge that the park had a reputation as a gay hangout, a place where married guys and hustlers met for illicit encounters.

Alex tried to shake off the sense of foreboding that was growing in him. So what if they weren't going for coffee. Maybe Cameron wasn't comfortable being . . . inside. Alex sat in the car with the engine off. He could feel the heat fading but he refused to turn on the engine again. He didn't want to do anything to make himself more conspicuous.

It took a minute for his eyes to adjust after he turned off the headlights. He tried to focus on what he could see of the forest outside. It was filled with ferns and old cedars and rhododendrons just barely illuminated in the pale moonlight. The wet leaves sparkled. The park was in the middle of town, but was dead quiet under the white noise of the brimming river that lay beyond the parking lot.

He sat for almost fifteen minutes, waiting, unable to shake the sense that there was something wrong with the whole situation: the parking lot, the older men walking by who stared in at him for a few seconds too long. Thoughts of Cleo and how she'd feel about this nagged him, as did thoughts of Chris. Not that Chris was anything more than a friend. An acquaintance, really.

Finally he heard the slice and rattle of skateboard wheels on wet pavement. Cameron loomed up out of the darkness and appeared at the driver's side window. In one smooth movement, he kicked his skateboard into his hand and pushed his black hair out of his eyes while Alex rolled down the window.

"Hey," Cameron said.

On the drive over, Alex had imagined the conversation they'd have. He'd tell Cameron about his riding, about his dad and Ms. Reed. About Detroit and Ms. Reed's thinly veiled threats to take the horse, his dreams of becoming a professional dressage rider. Cameron would nod and ask insightful questions. Then Cameron would talk about his problems and dreams while Alex listened. They'd stop somewhere for a good dinner. The dream filled Alex with a longing he hadn't felt since he'd first developed his obsession with horses.

But the reality was a chilly disappointment—literally. Alex's hands and feet were numb and the two of them were as awkward as strangers.

"You want to get in?" asked Alex.

"Nah. Come on out."

Cameron backed up a couple of steps to let Alex out of the car. Alex turned and locked the driver's side, then followed Cameron out of the parking lot and onto a path. They pushed through wet branches and stepped over slender trees toppled by a wet, heavy snow that had fallen over Christmas, remnants of which lay in small patches. The boys walked until they reached a small sandy beach that faced only dense undergrowth on the other side of the river. The moon shone brightly off the water and the night suddenly felt warmer than it had.

Cameron put his skateboard down and gestured for Alex to sit on it.

"Want a beer? I got some in my bag."

Without waiting for an answer Cameron began to dig around in his backpack. He handed a can to Alex, then opened his own and drank it in a few long gulps. He was already opening a second one as Alex took his first reluctant sip. Beer reminded him of his father— the worst part of his father.

Alex looked at Cameron and was struck again by how such a handsome face could be so filled with shadows and secrets.

"So you and Cleo," said Alex. He hesitated. "You guys are . . ."

"Nothing," said Cameron. "We're nothing."

Without seeming to move, he moved his hand onto Alex's. Alex could feel the warmth through his glove. There was a rustling noise behind them. Cameron retracted his hand as though he'd been burned.

An overweight man stepped out of the shrubs and stood in front of them. A gold wedding band glinted on his left hand. Alex couldn't see him very well but the man managed to ask the question without saying a word.

Alex shook his head and the man melted away, wandering off along the dark path.

For a moment Alex couldn't speak. When he finally found his voice he said, "We should probably go."

"He's harmless. Who knows, maybe he'd be good for a few bucks," said Cameron, before finishing off his second beer.

"What?"

"Just kidding," said Cameron, leaning back and smiling in a way that made Alex very uncomfortable.

Alex looked up and saw a cloud passing beneath the moon.

He struggled to find the words for what was bothering him. It wasn't just his feelings of guilt about Cleo. It was that he was in the lurker park with fat, married guys cruising him. He was with someone who called him "buddy." This wasn't at all how he'd envisioned his first date.

"What are we doing out here?" he asked.

"Hanging out," said Cameron, who gave him a look that made his brain freeze and his stomach burn. Alex resisted the temptation to let the feeling take him away.

"No. I mean us. Are we—?"

"Are we what?"

"Is this a date?"

The disgusted expression on Cameron's face made Alex flinch.

"You sound like a girl, man," said Cameron.

Alex knew then that whatever this was, it wasn't going any further than the park. He also knew this park wasn't enough for him—not now, not ever.

He got up and brushed himself off.

"Where are you going?"

Alex looked down and felt anger slice through him at whatever or whomever had sentenced Cameron to the dark.

"You should tell Cleo," he said.

Something shifted in Cameron's face for a moment and then the mask slipped back into place.

"Come on," he said. "Where are you going?"

"I mean it. You need to tell her."

"Tell her what?"

"That you're not that into her." *Because you're not into girls.* "Either you tell her or I will."

As Alex walked away he felt himself bracing for an attack that never came.

PHASE III

Riding the horse in greater collection with regularity, suppleness, and proficiency, and with an increased bend in the joints of the hind legs in all ordinary paces and jumps that can be copied from nature. These movements developed by training to the highest perfection are called High School. . . . The art of riding must be divorced from all mystery by simplicity and truth. High School will then be possible and free from all false doctrines and medieval conceptions, so that riding may again be acknowledged as an art within the reach of every serious rider.

—Alois Podhajsky, *The Complete Training of Horse and Rider in the Principles of Classical Horsemanship*

Alex

WHEN ALEX LED Detroit out of his stall at the Mid-Island Spring Horse Show, he felt a wash of embarrassment as people did double takes upon seeing Detroit's show sheet. Grace had told him that, as his sponsor for the show, she wanted to advertise her company name, so over the top of his winter stable blanket, Detroit wore a purple blanket made of two bedsheets Grace had sewn together. On either side she'd written "Graceful Hair Designs" in elaborate lettering. The logo was heavily accented with rhinestones. She'd thought long and hard about whether to add "Ltd.," but in the end decided that to do so would misrepresent her skills. "There's nothing limited about me," she'd concluded as she admired her handiwork.

When Cleo saw the show sheet, she told Alex that it probably wouldn't be necessary for him to come out formally. "That blanket'll make the announcement for you." Alex had been thinking about coming out a lot in the past few days. He and Chris had spent four afternoons together working on the music and Alex found himself increasingly fascinated by his friend.

Chris seemed to disappear into the task of designing the musical score for Alex's ride. He carefully watched the video of Alex riding his freestyle over and over while he played pieces of music he thought might match. He was as lost in the music as he was when he drew. Chris made music and art the way Alex rode: with complete absorption. Alex found it both comforting and inspiring.

Chris turned out to be right about the bhangra. The South Asian music was a perfect match for Detroit's elastic and athletic gaits. The music had strong rhythms and distinct beats, but it was also complex and full of surprises. It made Alex feel like dancing while twining scarves around himself. It made him feel like riding. When he tested it out, he was sure Detroit liked it, too. The big gelding lightened up and became more animated when the music played.

As Alex tacked up Detroit, he reflected that even though he was thrilled at the freestyle he and Chris had put together, he was confused and dismayed by his growing feelings for his friend. What could have been simple admiration for Chris's talent was amplified because Chris seemed interested.

During the four days they worked together, Alex had seen Chris looking at *him*. More than once. When he was tempted to make something of it, Alex remembered Cleo's delusion that his own occasional glance in her direction meant he was in love with her. Then he thought of the scorching looks Cameron had given him. Why did romance have to be so tangled and confusing? It would be hard enough if everyone wore a sign stating their preferences. It was practically impossible for someone who had no antenna for this stuff at all.

If Alex was a more confident person, he might have tried to raise the subject directly. Chris was a thoughtful, gentle person and Alex knew he'd be kind no matter how he felt. But Alex wasn't a confident person and kind wouldn't cut it. Quite the opposite. And Alex thought he would rather die than make

Chris uncomfortable or ruin their friendship. So he said nothing and pushed away his feelings.

"Do you need any help?"

Alex looked around and saw the person he'd just been obsessing about standing behind him. Blood rushed into his cheeks.

"Where's Sofia?" he asked out of habit.

"She's with your sisters and Grace. I think Sofia wants to join their gang."

Alex nodded. "They have that effect on people."

"You're all ready?"

"Actually, would you mind getting my show jacket? It's in there." Alex pointed at the small, walk-in dressing room at the front of Fergus and Ivan's horse trailer.

Chris came back carrying the coat and a plaid wool scarf. "It's kind of cold out. You might need this while you warm up." He held up the scarf. Alex, heart pounding, shrugged out of the heavy ski parka he wore over his pressed dress shirt and let Chris help him into his coat. When he finally had it on, Alex turned to his friend and began fastening the buttons with hands that should have been frozen but instead were strangely hot. When Chris very gently reached to put the scarf around Alex's neck, their hands met.

It was only a moment, but when it was over, Alex was suddenly eight feet tall and made of sunlight.

Grace told him later that the music seemed to take the small crowd by surprise. Alex didn't notice. As soon as he entered the arena everything disappeared but the horse and the music. As he rode down the centerline he felt Detroit's footfalls perfectly match the beats. They made a perfect transition to a square halt at *X*. Silence fell for a beat, two beats, three beats. Then the music began again, louder now, as Alex pushed Detroit off at a collected trot.

It seemed to Alex that he could feel the horse's back muscles ripple in time with the music as they crossed the diagonal at a medium trot. Detroit did a traverse to the right and then to the left at the trot, maintaining his rhythm. When Alex tightened his stomach, Detroit stopped in time with the crescendo. The horse backed up the four steps at the slightest prompt and then moved off again. Alex put the big gelding into a canter, again perfectly timed to the music. He lengthened and collected the horse's canter, then let him stretch his neck down to take the bit.

Alex felt as if he'd grown wings and that his horse was stepping on clouds rather than sand. The music swirled around them and Alex heard the crowd clapping in time. He put the horse into a medium trot and the clapping seemed to hold them aloft each stride for an extra moment.

When it was over and Detroit stood perfectly still and square at *X*, the music faded from the air, and several people in the crowd stood up and applauded.

Maybe it was just a schooling show and not an Olympic qualifier, and a second-level freestyle rather than a grand prix test, but Alex couldn't help feeling elated. He'd just spent over five minutes in the zone, that rare state of grace in riding when everything comes together. Time in the zone was elusive and generally measured in fractions of seconds, not entire minutes.

As soon as Alex and Detroit got out of the ring they were surrounded by people: coaches, sisters, friends. People he'd never spoken to before came over to congratulate him on a nice ride.

"Thanks," he said, careful not to let his excitement look like arrogance.

Fergus and Ivan were overcome with emotion, as

though Alex were a baby bird who'd just landed safely after his first flight.

"Lovely, my dear," said Fergus after he swung the woolen quarter sheet over Detroit's rump. "Just lovely. I admit I wasn't sure about that music, but by God it worked."

Ivan nodded. "That was good," he said.

"We were dancing along!" said Maggie. "Did you see us?"

Alex saw Ivan look down at his sisters, his white eyebrows knitted together.

"I've got to walk him out," he said, kicking his legs out of his stirrups and swinging a leg over the saddle.

When he hit the ground sharp pains shot through his feet as the full weight of gravity grabbed him again.

"Where's Cleo?" he asked, realizing he hadn't seen her since she went off to ride her first test. That was at least an hour ago.

Fergus shook his head and Ivan looked away, his lips pursed.

"What?" pressed Alex. His coaches didn't answer.

Alex gave up and walked over to Chris, who held out his winter jacket.

"Thanks," he said.

"Let me get a picture," said Grace. Chris tried to step out of the frame but she stopped him. "I want all of you."

Soon she'd herded Fergus, Ivan, Maggie, May, Chris, Sofia, and a couple of surprised strangers into a huddle around Detroit.

When she'd gotten her picture and the crowd had gone their separate ways, Alex turned to Grace.

"Have you seen Cleo?"

"I think there was a bit of a problem with her first ride."

"I saw Fergus and Ivan getting mad at her," said Maggie. "Something about drinking."

"Drinking?" asked Alex, feeling completely lost.

"Something about her drinking and not being allowed to ride in the rest of the show."

After Alex had cooled Detroit and put him in his stall he headed toward the jumper area to find Cleo. He figured the first person she'd run to was that reprobate roommate of hers.

He stood on the narrow gravel road that separated the rings from the barns as he decided whether to check the jumper ring or the jumper barn first. That's when he saw the champagne-colored Lexus.

His stomach dropped. The car was empty. Ms. Reed was here somewhere.

He quickly turned toward the jumper barn, choosing it because it was farthest from Ms. Reed's car, but before he could get very far Ms. Reed stepped out from behind a truck like she'd been waiting for him.

"Hello," she said. Her cheeks were flushed in the cold. Alex hadn't seen her for at least two weeks. In those two weeks his father had come home to his RV every night after work and stayed home on weekends. Alex had a sick feeling about the whole thing. His throat was suddenly so dry he couldn't swallow.

"I saw your little performance," said Ms. Reed.

Alex nodded cautiously.

"Watching you out there made me realize how much I miss riding," she said. "Especially since I have a bit more time on my hands these days. You know, since your father and I have stopped seeing each other."

They stared at each other for another long beat.

"Does your father know you're gay?" she asked without preamble. "No. I'm sure he doesn't. Brian doesn't see anything he doesn't want to. He doesn't see that your tramp of a mother is never coming back or that his precious son bats for the wrong team. Although personally, I don't know how he could miss it.

"Anyway, like I said, you've inspired me to take up riding again. It's time for me to start working with my own horse again. You can bring him home next weekend," said Ms. Reed. She stared at Alex for a long beat, then turned and walked away.

Alex stood rooted to his spot for a long minute. Then, in a fog of shock, he went off to find Cleo.

22

Cleo

I ADMIT THAT mistakes were made.

Mistake Number 1: Getting sent to Canada for crimes against vases and other household things.

Mistake Number 2: Signing up with elderly and unpleasant dressage coaches who lack the ability to relate to the demanding social requirements of a vibrant young person such as myself.

Mistake Number 3: Riding in close proximity to the unbearably focused and hardworking Alex Ford.

Mistake Number 4: Having a few drinks with Jenny before my first class at the Mid-Island Spring Show, which was scheduled at the unreasonable hour of eight-thirty A.M.

Mistake Number 5: Getting eliminated from my

first class of the day. Due to being a bit under the weather, sobrietywise.

I was sitting outside Tandava's stall, still trying to sober up when Jenny walked over.

She looked quite fresh considering she'd been up all night (I know because I was with her) and considering that she's the one who gave me a couple of drinks this morning to help "settle my stomach." Pre-ride drinking might work for jumpers, but it sure doesn't work for dressage.

"What are you doing?" she asked.

"I'm being punished."

She flashed a grin at me. "Did you run over the judge or something?"

"I kind of went off course."

"Big deal," she said. "I get eliminated for being off course practically every time I ride. It keeps things interesting."

"Not according to Fergus and Ivan."

"Oh well, stage a dramatic comeback during your freestyle this afternoon. That'll get you in the good books again."

I snorted and half the blood vessels in my head threatened to burst. "They only have one good book and it's full of Alex," I said.

She nodded. "Yeah, he's an awesome rider. I watched his test earlier. He's got a seat to die for."

"Well, he's all about the hard work," I said, making it sound like a bad thing. "Practice, practice, practice. Work, work, work. Try, try, try."

"That's inconsiderate of him," said Jenny.

"Don't I know. Anyway, don't you have a class soon?" I asked.

She smoothed her hands along her head and down the length of her ponytail.

"I've got an exchange student grooming Rio for me. And getting her warmed up."

I made a mental note to find an exchange student to exploit. I'd have to convince Fergus and Ivan, but that would have to wait until they calmed down and started speaking to me again.

A few minutes after Jenny left, Alex walked up. I could smell the focus coming off him, not to mention the clean leather, the shampooed hair, and the subtle aftershave. I couldn't see him, however, since I had my forehead resting against my knees.

"Cleo?"

"Yeah," I replied into my kneecaps.

"What are you doing?"

That got me to look up. "What do you mean?"

His face was super stern, like a disappointed Grade Five teacher, or like my dad after the Chad episode.

"What's going on with you? I heard you rode a terrible test. And you were a mess this morning," he said.

"Jeez, what would I do without your unconditional support?"

"You're going to ruin your breeches."

I was sitting in a mix of sand, dirt, and sawdust in my white show breeches, with my back against the wall. Alex didn't offer to help as I shoved myself up and then slumped into the folding chair.

"Have you been drinking?" he asked.

"You mean since last night?"

"Were you drinking this morning?"

I tried to make a dismissive noise but it sounded more like a baby spitting up.

"I may have had a bit of a hair of the god this morning."

"Hair of the dog."

"That too."

"What were you doing last night?"

"I went to a party in Nanaimo with Jenny. I was

hoping to see R— I mean Cameron again."

His face got even more disapproving. What was his problem?

"Did you?" he asked.

"Did I what?"

"See Cameron."

"No, but that doesn't mean anything. We're still seeing each other."

Alex stared at me, his brown eyes unreadable.

"I don't think . . ." He stopped and exhaled deeply.

"As far as I'm concerned, you think too much," I said. "Don't criticize me for having a love life just because you're so far in the closet you can't even find the door."

He winced and I felt a prickle of guilt.

"Cameron's not the right guy for you. That's all I'm trying to say."

"How do you know? Have you ever had a relationship that wasn't with a horse? Have you even had a real friend your own age? You're so obsessed with riding that there's no room for people in your life."

He hesitated, then said, "Cleo, Cameron's gay."

"Shut up. You wish."

"Cleo, he is."

"How would you know?"

"I just know."

Jealous. He was just jealous. God, he was sounding more like my dad every minute.

"Cameron and your friend Jenny don't—"

I cut him off. "Care about me? Give me a break. You're just jealous and it's pathetic. You can't stand that I might be popular."

"Jealous? Of a spoiled, selfish little—"

I was gone before he could finish. I heard him call after me, but I kept going until I couldn't hear anything anymore.

The thing is that I've heard it all before. Spoiled and selfish, all of it.

After the detective caught Chad and me together, he called my dad, who came and got me. He was by himself. My mother was in a meeting and couldn't get away.

I went and sat in the car while the investigator spoke to my father. While I waited for him it occurred to me that it was the first time my dad ever picked me up for anything. I must have smiled at the thought, because when he got into the car he told me to wipe the smile off my face.

"You're just lucky I was available to pick you up,"

he said, turning the car around jerkily. *No wonder he always uses a driver*, I thought.

"Look, Dad, I'm sorry you had to hire an investigator," I said.

"We didn't hire anyone. The insurance company did. You've made us look like damn fools." Should have known better than to think that my parents cared enough to hire an investigator.

"You want to tell me what the hell happened? The investigator says that you gave the guy access to our house."

"It wasn't like that," I said, suddenly wishing my mom or even Consuela had come to get me.

"We're going to the police station. Where the hell is the nearest one?"

He drove faster and faster. I was clinging to the door handle. I was afraid to take my eyes off the road.

"Stop it. Slow down. I don't need . . . I don't want to go to the police station."

"This guy, this driver, this Chad. Did he do something to you?"

"No!"

My dad gunned the car through a red light a second before it turned green. My words finally seemed to reach his brain and he slowed the car, wrenched the steering wheel to the side, and pulled over to the shoulder of the road.

"What?"

"He didn't do anything to me."

"You *wanted* him to rob our house?"

"Chad and I . . ." I stopped. *We were playing a sexy little game* wasn't going to cut it.

"You think this guy cares about you?" my father demanded.

I didn't reply. My face burned.

"He doesn't. He doesn't give a shit about you. You're just a spoiled, selfish little—"

"I didn't mean to," I said. "You don't have to get the police."

"You're right," he said. "We're not going to the cops, because you aren't worth the bad press or the hassle."

He pulled back out onto the road and drove us home to the empty house. The next day my parents were gone when I woke up. A month later I was on my way to Stoneleigh.

Closure, O'Shea style.

Cleo

I FOUND JENNY lying on her horse in the warm-up ring.

"Hey," I said, leaning up against the fence. I was trying not to cry, so it seemed like a good idea to keep words to a minimum.

"Ugh," said Jenny.

"Are you riding soon?"

She sat up and stretched her arms to the sky.

"I suppose so," she said.

"Jenny!" barked a voice. "Get that mare moving. Now!"

I looked over to see Stoneleigh's head coach, Vanessa Pringle, stride into the ring. Coach Pringle was probably in her midthirties, but working at

Stoneleigh had aged her. She had one of those figures people call boyish and she always seemed right on the verge of having a coronary, like a big-league football coach. If anyone could use a day-long spa treatment, it's her. As she walked into the middle of the ring, she swept her cap off her head. Her short hair was crushed against her scalp. She brushed it back a couple of times, then jammed the hat back on her head.

"Have you moved this horse at all?" she asked Jenny.

Jenny grinned down at her. "I didn't carry her into the ring."

"Smart-ass. Have you warmed her up?"

"Felicity did."

"I don't want to know," said Coach Pringle. "For God's sake, at least walk her around until it's your turn so she doesn't tear something."

Jenny saluted languidly and moved Rio off in a slow-motion walk.

Coach Pringle came and leaned against the fence near me.

She looked at me briefly. "You're the one with the big Holsteiner mare. You ride dressage."

I nodded.

"Bloody nice horse," she said. "You ever jump her?"

I shook my head.

"Those two," she said, gesturing at Jenny, who was now listlessly trotting her horse around, "are a disaster. Lovely horse, talented rider, both headed straight into the crapper."

She watched as Jenny took Rio over a jump that was at least chest level, then brought her back to a walk.

"You know, if you were my kid, I'd tell you to be careful around that one," said Coach Pringle, letting her gaze rest on Jenny, who was slumped in the middle of the ring again. "You don't want to get mixed up in her scene. Trust me on that."

"Yeah, thanks," I said, even though I knew it was too late.

I watched part of Jenny's ride but after they barely cleared the huge second jump I started to feel dizzy and had to leave. I was practically hypothermic, so I went and stood by my car, which Jenny has nicknamed the Soccer Mom Mobile. I couldn't bring myself to get into it.

I don't know when I've ever felt so lost, although

to my knowledge, I've never really been found.

What was I doing?

I was still standing there ten minutes later when Frieda walked up.

"Cleo," she said in her husky voice. Frieda's one of Jenny's friends. With her wild, curly hair she stands about seven feet tall. Frieda is the coolest girl at Stoneleigh. She doesn't ride and she never attends classes. All she does, as far as I can tell, is look good. She has this effortless, just-rolled-out-of-bed-with-a-rock-star-at-the-Chelsea-Hotel look we are all aiming for.

"Whatcha doing?" she asked. Her navy pea coat was unbuttoned, her inexpertly knitted scarf so long it nearly brushed the ground.

"I have no idea," I said.

"Come on." I turned and followed her back toward the rings.

Jenny and Rio stood just outside the jumper ring. Coach Pringle was talking to Jenny and gesturing unhappily.

"What the hell were you doing in there?" Coach Pringle yelled.

I couldn't hear Jenny's reply.

"I know you don't think I'm serious, but you're

wrong," blared Coach Pringle.

"Uh-oh," said Frieda in this very unconcerned way.

As we watched Jenny get chewed out, I heard someone near us grumble, "Those private school bitches think they're all that. Half of them can't even ride their fancy horses."

I turned to see who had spoken. A small group of riders in post-ride sweats and coats stood off to one side. I was glad my uniform was hidden under my duffel coat, but Frieda turned and fixed the girl with eyes like laser beams. Her untamed hair was electric and her long, slim neck made her look like an angry swan.

"What did you say?" she asked.

The girl who'd spoken blushed and stepped back behind her friends.

"Maybe they're stoned, eh?" whispered another girl in the group, making a play on the name of our school that was only funny when we said it.

Just then Jenny walked up leading Rio, and the potential rumble was averted.

"Cleo, my man, I need a drink," said Jenny as she handed me the reins.

I looked over to see Frieda still glaring at the girls.

Jenny didn't seem to notice or care. "Come on, ladies," she said. "Let's go get wasted."

Frieda and Jenny stalked off like two noble-women who'd just come off a foxhunt. I followed, leading Rio. Like a stablehand.

"Cleo, hon. Rio goes in there," said Jenny, pointing to a stall with the Stoneleigh Academy white-board hung on the front. Most of the other Stoneleigh signs had the horse and owner names as well as emergency contact information printed on them. The stall Jenny pointed to had only the school name. Jenny hadn't filled out Rio's information.

"Frieda and I are just going to take care of some business. We'll be back in a few minutes."

Then Jenny and Frieda disappeared and left me holding Rio.

I led the leggy chestnut mare into her stall, untacked her, and put her cooler on. I carried her saddle and bridle and splint boots over to the Stoneleigh trailer and got her a flake of hay. I filled her water bucket. Then I found the messiest and worst organized grooming box, guessing that it was Jenny's. As I worked I felt virtuous and a little self-righteous. I reflected that this must be how Alex feels all the time. I wondered who was taking care of my horse. Well, obviously, Alex was. He and Fergus and Ivan. They would never let anything happen to Tandava.

Rio stood between me and the door to the stall as I brushed her. I could hear some of the other girls from school coming back from their rides.

"Holy near-death triple," one girl said as she led her horse into the stall beside us.

"No shit," said another.

"I'd love to know why they have to make every course as complicated as possible."

I smiled. Doesn't matter what discipline you ride. Complaining is a language all horse people speak. I felt warm and safe in the stall with Rio as she peacefully munched her hay.

"You see those girls talking to Frieda?"

"Frieda was here?"

"Yeah. She was waiting for Jenny."

Somebody muttered something I couldn't hear.

"What?" said someone else.

"It's no wonder the locals are throwing us attitude."

"What do you mean?"

"Frieda and Jenny are hard-core, man."

Another mumble.

"Jenny's okay."

"Jenny can't remember a jump course to save her life. She's going to ruin that horse."

Abruptly the voices stopped and I heard footsteps come toward Rio's stall.

I stayed absolutely still in the shadows of the corner as someone looked in.

The footsteps retreated and the voices continued, "Come on, we all know she's gone over to the dark side."

"Don't exaggerate. She just likes to party."

"If that's what you want to call it."

"English, please."

"She's been doing the big H."

"Shut up."

"For real."

"So what, she's like some IV drug user now? A junkie?"

"I don't know if she's doing needles, but she's definitely smoking it."

"Jenny's a bit of a lush puppy, but she's not a . . . a smacker."

"I believe the term is *smackhead*. And yes, she is. Rachel saw her doing it at a party."

"You gonna tell Coach?"

"Are you kidding? She's already on the verge of kicking Jenny off the team."

"Damn. I was hoping we'd win this year. It's not going to happen if our top rider's some addict. Anyway, why couldn't she get addicted to something that's at least performance enhancing?"

"Like Christopher Jones. He's a coke fiend and he won a World Cup."

"You should suggest it to her."

They all laughed.

"'Course, he got caught and now he's suspended for life."

"Details, details."

"Hey, you should probably check and see if Rio has some food. Jenny never even brushes that horse anymore. It's a miracle she's still on four legs."

"Totally neglected."

I moved farther into the dark corner of the stall behind Rio when someone walked over and looked in.

"Yeah, she's eating. She'll be fine."

While the other Stoneleigh girls laughed and joked and put their horses away, I huddled in the corner, trying not to make any noise.

24

Alex

HE'D BEEN WALKING Detroit in the field behind the indoor arena for almost an hour when Chris found him.

"Is everything okay? You've been walking around back here for quite a while now. You're missing the rest of the show."

"It's fine," said Alex. He knew he sounded irritable. Impatient.

Chris pushed his hands deep into the pockets of his parka.

"When you get finished, do you want to do something? You know, later. With me and Sofia, or . . ." Chris hesitated. "Or just me."

Alex wanted to face Chris and tell him about

everything. That he'd lost his horse and his best friend. But he was afraid that if he started he'd break wide open. He couldn't handle any more attachments. He didn't want any kindness or pity. He didn't want any risk. So he kept walking as he spoke.

"No. I've got to go home." He kept his eyes on Detroit so he wouldn't have to see Chris's reaction.

There was silence for a moment and Alex knew Chris was waiting for him to say something, but he kept quiet. Eventually Chris said, "You know, Alex, I . . ." He stopped.

Alex looked up.

"I'm your friend," he said. "If you want to talk."

Friend, thought Alex. *Great.*

"I'm fine. See you later," said Alex.

Chris bit his lip and then turned and walked back toward the road. Alex watched him go. He was too cold to feel the regret he knew was coming.

For once, Fergus and Ivan looked their ages. Alex knew it was because one of their students had gotten drunk and abandoned her horse at the show and the other was nearly catatonic after losing his horse to a vindictive owner.

"Damn," muttered Fergus, who was behind the

wheel. "Damn. Damn. Damn."

Ivan just stared out the window.

"It's okay," said Alex from the backseat. "I mean, I don't think Ms. Reed's going to send Detroit for dog food or anything."

No one laughed.

After several minutes Fergus spoke. "You had a lovely ride today," he said.

Alex cleared his throat and blinked quickly.

"I know this . . . this business with Ms. Reed is disappointing," continued Fergus. "The world's full of disappointments."

Ivan made a rude, snorting sound from the passenger seat.

"What?" asked Fergus.

"Bah," said Ivan. "He doesn't need the patitudes."

"*Platitudes*. And yes, this is precisely the sort of situation that calls for a platitude."

Alex smiled. Something about the exchange between the two men was making him feel better.

When they pulled into the Fords' driveway Fergus and Ivan got out and helped Alex unload Detroit. Tandava whinnied loudly as her companion backed out of the trailer.

"Thanks," Alex told his coaches, who stood shoulder

to shoulder in the failing afternoon light.

"You're okay, then?" said Fergus.

Alex nodded, too full of emotion to speak.

Fergus touched a hand to Alex's shoulder and Ivan nodded abruptly, then walked quickly back to the truck and got in. Fergus lingered another few seconds.

"You've got the horse for a few more days?"

Alex nodded.

"We'll see you tomorrow, then."

Then he got back into the truck, turned around, and pulled away. Alex waved them past. He could hear Tandava kicking in the trailer. When they were gone he noticed his father standing near his RV.

Alex was suddenly uncomfortably aware that Detroit was still sheathed in the purple sheet blanket with the glittery Graceful Hair Designs logo.

"Those two, they're your teachers?" said Mr. Ford.

Alex nodded.

"They got wives or anything?"

Alex didn't answer.

"Jesus, they're not like . . . *that*, are they?"

"I've got to put Detroit away," said Alex.

"I'm trying to talk to you here."

Alex started walking and his father followed.

When Alex reached the gate he led Detroit through and closed it between him and his father, locking himself inside the pasture with the horses.

"Well?" said Mr. Ford.

"Well, what?"

"Those guys, those fancy riding guys. They ever try to touch you?"

"What?"

"I saw them. One of them touched you."

"You don't see anything," said Alex. "Ms. Reed was right about that, anyway."

His father took a step closer and Alex could see the muscles in his jaw working. His eyes were clear and Alex realized that his father was sober.

"If you think I'm just going to let you . . ."

"It's not up to you."

"I don't want you going over there no more," his father said.

Blood roared in Alex's ears. He was glad for the fence, however flimsy, that separated them.

"Don't worry," he heard himself say. "I won't be riding over there any more because your *girlfriend* is taking back her horse."

"She said you, I mean, she made it sound like you were . . . like *that*." In the fading light Alex could see the pain and confusion on his father's face. All at once his own anger evaporated.

"I am," he said simply. "And it's not because of Fergus and Ivan. I just am."

His father took a step back, shaking his head. "I thought she was just mad because I told her it was over. Between us."

"Go back to your RV, Dad," Alex said as gently as he could. Then he turned and walked to the barn, leaving his father standing, slump shouldered, outside the fence.

Cleo

WHEN THE STONELEIGH jumping team went to watch the next class, a good decision maker might have decided it was time to jump ship. A clear-thinking, rational type probably would have thought, *Hmmm, it seems that my companions are on heroin and since I don't want to get involved in any movie-of-the-week-type situations, perhaps I'll just head back to school to do homework. Or watch TV. Or take part in any number of safe, legal things.* Unfortunately there were no clear-thinking people around to advise me.

So I pulled a chair in front of Rio's stall and waited for Jenny and Frieda. The longer I sat there, the more hard-core I felt. I started thinking that I knew how homeless people feel. Homeless drug addicts! They are cold. They are friends with criminals and addicts. They sit around a lot, waiting for the shelter to open.

My cheeks even started to feel a bit sunken, drug-chic style. After about twenty minutes I was half-expecting someone to come by and interview me for a gritty documentary about the seedy underbelly of the young equestrienne community.

What I tried not to do was to think about my horse, or about Alex or Fergus or Ivan. When Phillipa walked by with her parents, I looked away, pretending I hadn't seen her, so she wouldn't come over. It worked. She took a step toward me, then veered back on course and kept going. I felt bad until I realized that that's the kind of thing that happens to those of us in the hard drug scene. We lose friends.

I tried thinking about my life, but it was like diving into murky water. I attempted to draw some conclusions, but the only one that came was that I was so cold it was going to require heroin, PCP, magic mushrooms, and crack cocaine to get me warm again.

"Dude, you waited," said Jenny as she came around the corner of the barn. Even she sounded surprised at how dumb that was. The crowds thinned out. Most people were loading up their horses or watching the last few classes of the day while they waited to pick up the prizes they knew they'd won. The day felt spent, yet here I was, waiting around for something to start.

Jenny and Frieda had obviously been doing *something*. Their pupils were pinpricks and they were moving slowly. Their skin was kind of pasty and shiny. Whatever they'd been doing didn't help their looks much, but I still wanted to be a part of it.

"So what should we do?" I asked, and felt all my street cred instantly disappear. Not that I had any street cred to begin with, but I should have known enough to at least *pretend* I was indifferent.

Frieda exhaled noisily, as though I'd just asked an extremely complicated question.

Jenny stepped in. "The three of us have been working hard all day. I mean, Cleo and I got up at five-thirty after we went to bed at three. What we need here is some R & R. I thought we could head into town. Maybe check out a couple of parties. You okay with that?"

I nodded, my mind full of thoughts of Cameron. And Alex, that liar.

"Oh, okay. What about Rio?" As I said it, I felt a wave of guilt for abandoning Tandy. Oh well, Alex and Fergus would take care of her.

Frieda exhaled again, even more loudly this time.

"It's cool. I'll leave a note for one of the other girls to load her and put her away at school. She'll be fine," said Jenny.

"Won't Coach Pringle get mad if you don't head back with the rest of the team?"

"Cleo, my friend, you worry too much. Pringle'll just think I got a ride with you and your coaches."

The three of us began walking toward my car. Jenny and Frieda walked like they were knee-deep in mud. I had to keep slowing to let them catch up.

Once we were in the car, Jenny turned to me. "Hey, Cleo?"

"Yeah?"

"Have you got any cash?"

"No, my allowance doesn't come until next week."

"What about your credit card?"

"There's hardly any room left because I put a down payment for the car and some other stuff on it. Plus, I'm not allowed to get cash advances with it. My parents set it up like that."

"Shit," she said. "Okay. Then we're going to need to make one quick stop."

I looked from her to me. We were both still in our show clothes.

"Shouldn't we get changed?" I asked.

"Nooooo," complained Frieda from the backseat. "I just want to *get* somewhere. So we can *relax*."

"Don't worry, Soccer Mom," Jenny said to me. "Everyone is going to love your tight pants."

I turned the heat up as high as it would go, and pulled my new station wagon out of the parking lot.

Jenny asked me to pull over in front of a rundown house in the south end of Nanaimo. I stayed in the car and watched as Frieda and Jenny walked up some decrepit steps to a door covered in peeling gray paint. There were blankets hanging in the windows. It took about five minutes for someone to open up. A skinny guy started shaking his head as soon as he saw Frieda and Jenny. He stepped out onto the landing and looked up and down the street suspiciously.

Frieda and Jenny gestured at him, like they were pleading. Then Frieda turned and pointed toward the car. I ducked down as far as I could.

The thought flashed through my head that my roommate and her friend were trying to sell me into the white slave trade. They were arranging with scary drug guy to have my car jacked! Me murdered! I was not half hard enough for this scene. But my faulty decision-making skills again kicked into action and I continued sitting there.

Seconds later Jenny and Frieda were getting into the car.

"Dude. We need to go back to school," said Jenny.

"What? Why?"

"We need that stuff you bought for our room. You know, the leather stool thing and all that."

"And your iPod Nano," said Frieda. "That's sweet."

I couldn't believe it. They wanted to sell my things for drugs. This was even worse than Chad, that turd, stealing our furniture. I mean, at least that was my parents' stuff. This was mine. Bought with my parents' money, but still. I bought it for *us*.

"Cleo. It's for the *cause*," said Jenny.

"Take one for the team, babe," said Frieda.

"Look, I don't know."

"We'll get it back," said Jenny, outright lying to me now.

"Think of it like a bargaining chip," added Frieda.

I sighed and started the car.

A half hour later we were back at the shitty old house and Jenny and Frieda had carried my DVD player, my iPod and speaker, and my leather stool inside. They wanted me to give up my laptop, too, but

I told them my parents would freak. In truth, all I'd have to say is that I dropped it. My parents would never know the difference. I didn't do it, though. I was worried about how many drugs a laptop would buy. I didn't want Jenny and Frieda to OD or anything.

This time they left me sitting in the car for what seemed like hours. Darkness crept down the street and people began to appear on the cracked old sidewalks. A couple of young guys in baggy shorts and oversized down-filled coats sat on low-rider bicycles in front of a run-down convenience store on the corner.

"Hurry up," I whispered. The car kept losing heat, so every few minutes I had to start it up and let the heater run, doing my part to contribute to global warming.

When Jenny and Frieda finally came out of the house they smelled like cat pee, and instead of being all slow and drowsy, they were hyper and twitchy. They started talking as soon as they got their car doors open. I had this strong sense of being the woman in charge. The person in control. The soccer mom.

"Okay, okay, Cleo. We didn't forget you. We're going to go to a party."

"It's going to be so fun," said Frieda. "So fun. So, so fun."

Sober and stiff from sitting in the cold car, I started the engine.

"I really think we should get something to eat," I said in my best Cleo-in-Charge voice.

"Are you kidding?" Jenny squeaked.

"Eww! No," said Frieda, from the backseat. "No, no, no."

I followed Jenny's directions and drove us out of the south end and up toward Westwood Lake. We parked in the driveway of a house in the middle of a subdivision so new that the front yards were just dirt. All the houses looked identical in the dark. It was only about seven o'clock, but felt much later. There was only one other car in the driveway of the house.

I followed Jenny and Frieda up to the front door, wishing, as we went, that I was somewhere else. Anywhere else, actually. I comforted myself with the thought that maybe Cameron would be here. He was cute and he made me laugh. He didn't say much, but I knew he was into me and that was enough. I had already planned how I would tell him what Alex had said and how he'd reassure me that Alex must be on the pipe even more than my companions. Then we'd make out.

A woman wearing tight jeans and a lot of eyeliner

answered the door. Her face was tense and hard and her bleached hair was tangled up in a banana comb.

From what I could see, the house was basically empty. One little love seat sat by itself in the middle of a beige, carpeted living room. There were no pictures on the sand-colored walls. Most of the lights were off. I saw no sign of a party.

Jenny stayed upstairs to talk to the woman and I followed Frieda downstairs. The cat pee smell I'd detected on Jenny and Frieda was even stronger in the basement. It was making my eyes water. A couple of candles gave off the only light. As my eyes adjusted I could see kids sitting on couches, sitting on the floor, leaning against the walls.

I've watched enough TV to know a drug den when I see one, and this was definitely a drug den.

I stood like an idiot, staring at the people on the couch, who were passing something back and forth. It looked like a glass pipe. I wondered what they were serving for dinner at school. I wondered how I was going to get out of here.

"Here," Frieda whispered like we were in church. She put a beer into my hand and pushed me in the direction of an empty chair.

"Is this the party?" I whispered back.

"Shhh," said Frieda, and then she moved away from me and knelt down in front of a group of people on the couch who were all staring at something on the coffee table. Drugs. They were staring at drugs.

I wondered if the drug lord guy would keep my iPod and listen to it. If he did, would he like the songs I had on there? Was he a Jack Johnson fan? He didn't look like one, but you never know.

To stop myself from (a) dying of hunger and (b) wondering anything else, I drank my beer as fast as I could. I just wanted to relax, get into the party atmosphere. Well, maybe not *completely* into it. I wasn't going anywhere near that pipe. At least not right now.

Frieda got up and gave me another drink and pointed to a wall against which several cases of beer were stacked. No one else seemed to be drinking.

I got the third beer for myself because Frieda was busy at the coffee table.

A light opened up at the top of the stairwell and blinked out again when the door closed. A few seconds later Jenny crouched down beside me.

"You find him?" she whispered.

"Who?"

"Your guy. He's supposed to be here."

I shook my head, feeling dizzy.

When I got up to get another beer, I tried not to stare at Jenny and Frieda as they huddled around the coffee table with the other couch people. Jenny's breeches shone white in the candlelight. There was some electronic music playing, but it was very faint.

I had to go to the bathroom, so I got up and went looking in the direction I'd seen a couple of other people head. One door opened to small room containing a washing machine and dryer.

The second door opened up to a bedroom. There was a twist of movement in the darkness as I opened the door. Two people. I couldn't see their faces, but I knew instantly that one of them was Cameron. The other was some man. I stood, frozen in the doorway. Then Cameron picked something off the floor to shield the whiteness of his body. The man stared back at me, his eyes the only true black in the room.

"Oh," I said. Then I turned and ran.

I went up the stairs two at a time. Jenny called after me, but I didn't slow down.

I crossed to the front door of the house in about two strides. Then I was puking on somebody's lawn. When I finished, I got in the car, but couldn't get the keys to work because my hands were shaking and my eyes were watering. From the fumes. From the dark.

Finally the stupid Soccer Mom Mobile started and I took off. From the corner of my eye I saw a family come and stand in the brightly lit picture window of a house as I raced the car across their patch of dirt. Then I was gone.

I made it almost all the way down the hill, part of the time on two wheels. I might even have managed to make the turn-off to Jingle Pot Road if the telephone pole hadn't gotten in the way. One minute I was flying through the dark in the Soccer Mom Mobile and the next there was a pole buried in the hood of the car. The shriek of crumpling metal seemed to come a second after the impact and the soft boom of multiple air bags hit me with satisfying violence, leaving me suspended between them, my nose dripping red all over the white plastic.

Two cops drove me to the station after the paramedics checked me out and realized that my only injuries were a bloody nose and what would soon be two very black eyes. When I was being pulled out of the ruined Passat my first thought was that I'd never had so many good-looking men paying attention to me all at once. The fire department was there, and between them, the cops, and the paramedics I had what amounted to a trifecta of uniformed hotness around me. I was feeling pretty special, at least until I got a look in the interview room mirror at the police station and realized they were just doing their jobs and weren't necessarily overwhelmed by my beauty.

Officers Ray and Gonzales left me alone in the room for quite a while. They were probably letting me cool my heels. I've watched enough cop shows to know that's a very popular interrogation technique. Still, it only took about three seconds before I started to panic. I considered throwing myself on the ground and just lying there but realized that would probably get me a visit to the psych ward. *Equestrienne, Interrupted*.

I attempted to wipe the blood off my upper lip and chin but it was caked on. I used the wall-to-wall mirror to practice my impassive drinking-driver-being-interviewed-by-the-cops face. I tried a tough-unbreakable-repeat-felon face and a cooperative-and-concerned-citizen face before I realized that the mirror was probably two-way glass and officers Ray and Gonzales were probably sitting on the other side watching me audition faces. Not cool.

When they finally came back into the room, I'd

decided to act like a preteen Drew Barrymore at her lowest point. The idea was to be as cute and vulnerable as possible. I tried to arrange my face to suggest that I had a great future ahead of me if I could just get through this rough patch.

"Miss O'Shea. Are you still with us?" asked Officer Gonzales.

A trick question? I'd heard about those!

"Well, I haven't gone for coffee," I said, trying to bring some much-needed levity to the situation.

"We need you to focus here. Do you take drugs?"

I tried to look offended. "No!" I said. "I don't even smoke cigarettes." Although I'd been meaning to take up smoking to help pass the time while I waited for my druggie friends.

Officer Ray, a big guy with iron-gray hair and a large chin with a deep cleft in it, settled back in his chair, which groaned under his weight.

"You know that you blew just at the limit, right?"

I said a silent prayer of thanks that I'd thrown up right before I got in the car. Who knows what I'd have blown if all the beers had stayed in my system? The four of them probably added up to a third of my body weight.

"As a minor, you aren't allowed to have any alcohol

in your system when you drive. We've taken a blood sample and if we find anything else in there we can charge you with driving under the influence. As it is, you're definitely looking at a suspension."

I smiled at him as winningly as I could. Then I caught a glimpse of myself in the mirror. With blood all down the front of my coat and blouse and breeches and my two black eyes, I looked like a zombie that wanted to eat him. I stopped smiling and stared back down at the table.

"Where were you going in such a hurry?" asked handsome officer Gonzales.

I looked at him out of one eye. It would have been nice if we'd met under different circumstances. I considered mentioning that, then thought better of it.

I also considered telling them about the house and what was going on in the basement. I considered telling them about Jenny and Frieda. And about Cameron.

"Nothing. I wasn't going anywhere. I was just driving around. I go to Stoneleigh, the riding academy. I was on my way back to school."

"The school doesn't mind you driving around drunk in your parents' car?"

"It's my car."

The cops exchanged looks.

Clearly the wrong thing to say.

"Can I make a phone call?"

They exchanged another look. Officer Gonzales got up and headed for the door. Officer Ray sat solidly, staring at me.

"We're going to call your school. Get someone down here to pick you up."

"But don't I get a phone call?" I really didn't want them calling the headmistress.

"Officer Gonzales has gone to get you a phone."

We sat in silence for a long minute. I tried to casually rub some of the crusties off my nose. My lip was tender and I realized it was probably fat. At least I wasn't hungry anymore.

Officer Gonzales came back and put a portable phone on the table in front of me. The two of them watched as I dialed the number.

An hour and a half later Fergus and Ivan and I sat in Ms. Green's office. Ms. Green looked the same as she always does, even though it was almost ten o'clock at night. I'm starting to wonder about her relationship with that tweed suit.

"Thank you, Mr. O'Riley and Mr. Peev, for bringing

Cleo back after this . . . unfortunate incident."

"Yes, of course," said Fergus.

Ivan didn't speak, but every so often he reached out and patted the arm of my chair. Surprisingly something about his furniture patting was more comforting than most people's hugs.

"I'm terribly sorry that you and Mr. Peev were roused from your bed—" Ms. Green stopped talking and her cheeks colored.

"We run a barn, Ms. Green. We're always on duty," said Fergus.

"Well, thank you again for picking her up and bringing her back to school."

She obviously thought the meeting was over, but Fergus and Ivan didn't move. Ivan glanced quickly at Fergus, who spoke up.

"Ms. Green. We were just wondering, what happens now?"

"That's something I will be discussing with Cleo's parents. I really can't say, Mr. O'Riley."

"If there's anything we can do," said Ivan.

"Anything," echoed Fergus.

"This is a matter for the school and Cleo's parents."

"Of course."

"Thank you both very much," said Ms. Green, getting up from behind her desk to indicate that the meeting was over.

Fergus and Ivan rose at the same time. I just sat there. Fergus put a hand on my shoulder. "It'll be all right. We'll take care of your mare. You just get things straightened out with your parents. We'll see you soon."

Ivan air-patted me about a foot above my shoulder.

"For the time being Cleo will be confined to school property," said Ms. Green.

I got up out of my chair and watched Fergus and Ivan turn to leave the room. Then I remembered the monogrammed handkerchief Ivan had handed me as we left the police station to clean off my face.

"I've still got your kerchief," I said, holding up the formerly lovely square of fabric.

"You bring to the barn later," said Ivan.

In that moment, there was nowhere else in the world I wanted to go more.

26

Alex

AS ALEX RODE along the driveway to Limestone Farm on Sunday morning, he reflected that only a few hours had passed since the show and in that time his life had imploded. Or exploded. He wasn't sure which. Yesterday he was a serious dressage student and now he was faced with having no horse to ride. Yesterday he was his father's straight son. Today he was his father's shame.

Alex stopped Turnip for a moment so he could look out over the fields and the lake. The sky was clear and it was warm for early March. The air thrummed with life. Birds flitted from tree to tree and the sight of horses in pastures filled him with calm. He could sit and stare forever. Turnip and

Detroit seemed to feel the same way. They stood as still as statues on the hill.

Alex noticed some movement down at the barn. Someone walked quickly into the stable. It was unlike Fergus or Ivan to move so fast. They had the slow, deliberate movement of people who spend a lot of time around horses.

His curiosity aroused, Alex urged Turnip on. When he reached the barn, he dismounted and led both horses into an empty field. He removed Detroit's halter and quickly stripped Turnip of his saddle and bridle and turned him loose, too.

Both horses stood at the fence watching him, instead of going off to graze like they usually did.

In the barn Alex found Fergus standing outside Tandava's stall.

"It's about time," said Fergus. "Oh, I'm sorry, lad. I thought you were the bloody vet."

Worry was etched deep into Fergus's face. Alex walked a few steps closer.

"Is everything okay?"

Fergus shook his head.

Alex peered into the stall. Tandava lay on her side. Every so often her legs jerked, as though she were pawing at something no one could see. When she threw her head back Alex could see that the whites of her eyes had turned red.

Ivan crouched near the mare, staying well clear of her thrashing legs. He held the rope attached to her halter and whispered softly to her.

"What happened?" Alex asked.

"She's got a stomachache. She's colicking."

"Shouldn't we get her up? Walk her around?"

"Not when she's like this. When the vet comes he'll give her a shot. Something to help with the pain. Then we'll try again to get her on her feet."

Another spasm wracked the mare and her legs kicked. Alex could see her muscles straining.

"Jesus lord," said Fergus. "Where is that vet?"

Alex wanted to help but he didn't know how. He ran to the doorway of the barn and saw the vet's red truck coming down the hill.

"He's here," he called.

"Thank God," said Fergus. "Alex, you better take the truck and go get Miss Cleo."

Fergus handed Alex a set of keys and Alex nodded and ran toward the house, where the truck was parked.

He could hear Cleo's voice down the hallway.

"But Moooooom, I'm fine. It was just a misunderstanding. You don't need to tell Daddy."

Alex averted his eyes from all the girls in various stages of dress who stood in their doorways staring at him as he passed. He hadn't checked in with the office because he didn't want to waste any time.

He was glad to have Phillipa to lead him. He'd seen her on his way in and she offered to take him to Cleo's room.

When Phillipa knocked on Cleo's door there was no answer, just another cry of "Mooooommmm, Goooooodddd."

Phillipa turned the knob, pushed the door open an inch, and spoke into the crack. "Cleo, you've got a visitor."

"I'm on the phone," came the irritable reply. "I'm in trouble for something that is barely even my fault." Then she switched her attention back to the call. "I'm fine here. I don't need to go to school in Switzerland. And you *don't* need to tell Daddy."

Phillipa glanced apologetically at Alex and tried again.

"Cleo. I think it's an emergency."

"Look, I've got to go. Okay. Yeah, sure you will. No, I'm not trying to give you attitude. Never mind. Good-bye!"

A moment later Cleo appeared in the doorway and Alex took an involuntary step back. She looked like she'd gone the distance with Oscar De La Hoya. Her eyes were ringed with purple circles and her nose was swollen.

"What happened? Are you okay?" asked Alex and Phillipa in the same breath.

"I would be much better if everyone would stop asking that," said Cleo.

"Cleo, you need to come down to the barn."

"I'm on restrictions. I can't leave." She looked more closely at Alex. "Why? What's going on? Are Fergus and Ivan okay? Tell me I didn't give one of them a heart attack or something."

Alex shook his head. "It's Tandava."

Cleo narrowed her puffy, discolored eyes. "What's wrong with her?"

"You should come now. Get dressed and I'll drive you."

They stepped back and Cleo closed the door. Alex and Phillipa stood quietly for a long moment. Finally Phillipa spoke. "Is she bad? Tandava, I mean," she clarified, in case he thought she was asking about Cleo.

Alex nodded.

"Is she going to be okay?"

He shrugged. "They don't know. They can't get her up."

"That's awful," Phillipa said, her big eyes filling with tears.

When Cleo emerged from her room a few seconds later her face was pale with anxiety.

"I'll wait around here and cover for you if Ms. Green or anyone comes looking," said Phil.

"We should go," said Alex, and then he had to run to catch up with Cleo as she rushed down the hall.

27

Cleo

IF I WERE to be completely honest, I'd have to say that I never really thought about what horses and riding meant to me. Lessons used to mean I got to stare at the back of Chad's perfect head during long private car rides. In addition, I have always liked riding clothes, especially the tall black boots. I enjoy telling people that I ride. I guess the riding itself was okay, too, especially when I rode Dawn's very well-trained horses. Thanks to them, when I competed, I won, even though I wasn't all that great.

After I got Tandava and was sent to Stoneleigh, the thing I liked best about dressage was Alex and his family and Fergus and Ivan. I enjoyed watching Alex work hard. I got a kick out of how much he loved the horses, how much he loved riding, and how hard he tried. I loved watching him fuss around the barn. His enthusiasm was almost contagious, except for the working hard part.

I guess somewhere along the line I started to care about my horse. When I got to the barn this morning and saw how sick she was, how much pain she was in, it finally occurred to me that what I was supposed to love most about riding was her. The realization came as a sick shock, like *now you tell me*. How was I supposed to know? Plastic horses don't get stomachaches.

When Alex and I pulled up to the barn, Tandava was standing in the middle of the yard, her back legs stuck out stiffly behind her. Fergus held the lead rope and Ivan kept a steadying hand on her shoulder as the vet pulled a long tube out of her nose. Blood dripped steadily from her nose and splashed to the ground.

"She's had a shot to help with the pain and he's just given her a stomach tube to check for gasses and what's in her stomach," said Fergus as we walked up. "It must have started in the night. She was down when I came out to feed at six-thirty."

Ivan moved to let me stand beside her. I put my

hand on her damp neck. Her sides heaved rapidly, in and out.

"Don't get too close," said the vet, a tall, thin man in denim overalls. "She could go down like a ton of bricks. You don't want to get in the way."

Tandava's nostrils flared and then tightened. Every so often she swung her head around to look at her sides.

"Can you give her more pain medicine?" I asked. "Or something to calm her down?"

The vet shook his head.

"We don't want to give her a narcotic or a tranquilizer. She's in shock and her electrolytes are completely out of whack."

"Why is her nose bleeding?" I tried to control my shaky voice.

"The tube was a bit too big. I've made a note on her chart."

"Does she need surgery? Is she going to be okay?"

The vet stared at me. His eyes were serious.

"I don't know. She seems a little better now. You're going to need to walk her. Not so much that you tire her out. Keep listening for rumbling sounds in her belly. We want her to pass some stool so we know she doesn't have an impaction."

I nodded, glad to have Alex and Fergus and Ivan with me. "Okay. I can do that."

"Good," said the vet. "I've got an emergency about fifteen minutes away. I'll be back in a couple of hours to check on her. Call immediately if she gets any worse."

He spoke to me like I was in charge. Like Tandy was my responsibility. Which, it finally occurred to me, she was.

Then he put his instruments back in his box and his box in the back of his truck and drove off.

Tandava's pain seemed to come in waves. She would stand completely still, unwilling to move, like she was listening for some faraway signal. At other times she'd kick at her belly and bite her sides. I fell into a pattern of walking her once or twice around the indoor area and then standing with her in the middle of the ring. Every so often I put my ear to her side to listen for noises in her stomach.

"When it goes quiet you have to worry," Fergus said.

"You needing a break?" asked Ivan, after I'd been walking and resting her for a couple of hours.

"No, I'm fine," I said, but I was glad that he and

Fergus and Alex took turns keeping me company.

Partway through the afternoon, Tandy passed a bit of manure and we all celebrated like she'd just graduated from college.

"Now you want to take a rest? Go back to school? We can take care of her tonight," said Fergus.

I shook my head. I wasn't leaving the barn until I was sure Tandy was better. I was probably in deep trouble already for leaving school when I was on restrictions.

"Don't you have to ride Detroit?" I asked Alex as the afternoon wore on. He was religious about keeping up with his training schedule.

"No," he said.

"But you never miss Sundays. I'm sure Tandy's going to be fine. You can go ride."

"Detroit doesn't . . . he's not in training anymore."

"What?"

Alex cleared his throat. "Ms. Reed's taking him back next week. She and my dad broke up."

I felt my mouth fall open. All this time I'd spent with him today and he hadn't told me!

"Alex, I'm so sorry. About Detroit, I mean. Not your dad and Ms. Reed."

He shrugged.

"Is there anything I can do?"

He shook his head.

"I'm so sorry," I said again, because I couldn't think of anything else.

"I know," he said.

Around dinnertime Grace and Maggie and May showed up with pizza.

"Alex called and said you had a sick horse," said Grace. "I thought we'd bring over some local cuisine so we could make you sick, too."

Tandy was back in her stall. The vet had said it would be okay to give her a tiny bit of hay, but no grain. She was picking at her hay, but at least she was eating. I'd pulled a padded rope across the doorway instead of sliding the stall door shut, so I could see what she was doing. Every few mouthfuls Tandy lifted her head and looked right at me, like she was making sure I was still there. All the other horses were fascinated by the pizza party in the barn and I have to say it was a huge improvement over a lot of the parties I've been to recently.

After Grace and the twins left, I heard another car pull up. Alex went outside to see who it was and came back with Phillipa.

"Hey," she said. "I got Mrs. Mudd to drive me over."

My heart sank. She was probably here to tell me I was getting expelled and would be on the next boat to Switzerland.

"Am I suspended?" I asked.

"Your mom called back after you left and I told her what was going on. So she called Ms. Green. I don't know what she said, but Ms. Green said you could stay here as long as you need to."

"My mom probably promised to pay for the rest of the new indoor arena," I said.

"That's pretty cool," said Phillipa.

"Yeah," I said, because in a way it was. "Is Jenny back yet?"

"No. I heard Coach Pringle kicked her off the team because she was so out of it at the show and because she just ditched Rio and took off after. Which means she's kicked out of school, too."

"Oh."

"Is Tandy going to be okay?" Phillipa asked.

"Looks that way."

"I'm glad, Cleo."

Phil stood in the walkway, her thumbs hitched awkwardly in her jacket pockets.

"You want to hang out? Have some cold pizza?" I asked.

Phillipa smiled shyly. "Okay, sure."

Alex went and got another folding chair and we re-formed into a semicircle around Tandy's stall. We wrapped ourselves in horse blankets and talked quietly and sometimes didn't talk at all until we all fell asleep. As I fell asleep, surrounded by my friends in the quiet of the barn, I thought that when I get a real boyfriend, one who isn't gay or a criminal, I want one who would sit here with me, just like this. When I opened my eyes in the morning, the first thing I saw was Tandy, watching me. It was like she'd been watching me all night.

Cleo

THE DAY WE took Detroit back was like the day of a big funeral. The whole world seemed to speak in whispers. Alex and I went for a little ride around Limestone before we took Detroit back to Ms. Reed's. I rode Turnip while Alex rode Detroit. Tandava had recovered from her colic, but it hadn't mellowed her any. She's no trail horse.

After we rode every drenched path and trail on the property and filled our noses with the smell of leather and damp horse, Alex said he was ready. We stopped the horses outside the barn and Fergus and Ivan came out to say good-bye. Ivan patted Detroit and briefly tapped a finger on Alex's booted calf. It was Ivan's version of bursting into tears and giving him a hug.

Fergus's face was drawn and unhappy. He whispered something into Detroit's ear and then looked at Alex.

"So you're all set?"

Alex nodded. "Grace is going to drive his stuff over."

"I'm glad you brought him by for another hack around the place. We'll miss him."

Then Fergus ran out of words.

Alex moved Detroit off and I followed. We turned the horses up the driveway and into the shadows. After we hit Yellow Point Road, we rode in single file until we reached Cedar Road. In what seemed like no time we were at Ms. Reed's. A new, wrought-iron gate across her driveway was opened by a man I'd never seen before. He'd obviously been waiting for us.

"Ms. Reed's not home," he said. "I'm doing some, uh, landscaping for her. She told me you'd be coming and said that you were to put the horse in his pasture and leave his gear in the tack room." The man coughed, embarrassed. "She wanted to make sure all his stuff came back, so she gave me a list."

Alex was stone-faced. He swung out of the saddle and led Detroit toward the barn.

The man turned to me. "I'm sorry. I've got my instructions."

"Don't say anything else to him, okay?" I said. "Don't worry about the list. She'll get everything back. Someone will be here in a minute with the rest of it."

"Has it all been cleaned?" The man looked even more embarrassed. "She told me I had to ask."

"That horse's gear will never be this clean again," I said.

I held Turnip while Alex untacked Detroit and brushed him one last time. He was just finishing when Grace and the twins pulled up in the IROC. The landscaper waved them in, and I helped Grace and the twins unload Detroit's blankets and sheets and accessories, most of which Alex had bought for him in the few months he'd been riding the horse. Alex insisted they all belonged to Detroit now and should go home with him. Judging by the stacks of neatly folded blankets, Detroit had more clothes than Alex did.

When he was finished grooming the big horse, Alex put Detroit's new, bright-green winter rug on. The color was electric against the horse's gleaming bay coat. Then Alex led Detroit into his pasture and slipped off his halter. I snuck a glance at the twins. They were both in tears. I was afraid to look at Grace.

Detroit snuffled Alex's chest and then nudged at his pockets until Alex produced a treat. Then Alex walked out and closed the gate. When he reached us, I handed him Turnip's reins. His face was still a mask.

"I'll be home in a while," he said to no one in particular as he led the old paint down the driveway and out the gates. Detroit followed Alex and Turnip as far as he could and when he could go no farther, he began to whinny and trot back and forth, calling them back.

29

Alex

IT WAS FRIDAY night and Alex was wandering around the house, floating on a thick sludge of boredom and depression. Grace had taken the twins to kung fu and gone off to torture some poor woman's hair into shape, so he was on his own. His father was in his RV but he might as well have been on the moon for all he'd had to do with Alex in the few weeks since their little talk.

With Detroit gone, Alex found the hours stretched in front of him like years. *So,* he thought grimly, *this is what life is like for people who don't ride.*

The first couple of weekends he went to Limestone Farm to help out but it was obvious that Fergus and Ivan didn't really need him and he felt pathetic cleaning stalls because he had nothing better to do. Princess was too old to work, and seeing Cleo ride gave him pains in places he couldn't name.

Grace and Maggie and May did what they could to cheer him up. Grace cooked him several revolting dishes, which he pretended to enjoy, and she highlighted his hair, which he actually did enjoy. Maggie and May offered him the role of Man Who Gets Beaten Up in their new fifteen-minute film, *Murder at Deadwood Junior High*, but he didn't much care for being pummeled, even if it was in the service of art.

He brushed Turnip until Maggie pointed out that he was going to brush the old gelding's hair right off. He cleaned the small stable until it gleamed. He raked symmetrical lines into the shavings in Turnip's stall. He color-coordinated his brushes and transferred Turnip's pellets and supplements into attractive, matching plastic bins in graduated sizes.

He did homework.

And he thought constantly about calling Chris.

He hadn't told Chris or Sofia about losing Detroit. After he'd shut Chris out at the show, their friendship had slipped back into slightly awkward casual acquaintance territory. Sofia had recently been elected secretary general of the Model U.N. Club by several boys who had tremendous, knee-shaking crushes on her. When she was off at lunch practicing human-rights speeches and conflict resolution, Alex and Chris hung out together, but they barely talked. Chris sketched and listened to his headphones and Alex pretended to read. And every so often their eyes met and Alex felt a fresh wave of confusion.

Enough time had gone by that Alex was beginning to think he'd imagined the electricity that had leaped between them when Chris had helped him on with his scarf. He couldn't stop thinking about how he'd pushed Chris away when he needed him because he was too scared to be honest. Alex had begun Googling the bands he saw on Chris's T-shirts, telling himself that he'd be ready if Chris ever wanted to discuss the history of the Pixies or Radiohead or Sonic Youth.

Another wave of boredom washed over him. It was six-thirty P.M. Was that too early to go to bed? He tried to remember what he did before he got a horse. Oh, right. He used to ride his bike around and pretend it was a horse. He wandered into the garage and found Del Magnifico le Noir tucked away in his little corner. The blanket that covered the bicycle was dusty. Alex took it off and laughed when he saw that the red dog leash was still attached to the handlebars.

He rolled the bike back and forth a few times. It was so small. He glanced quickly around and then sat on it. He had to poke his knees out at almost right angles so they wouldn't hit the handlebars.

There wasn't enough room to ride in the garage, so Alex hit the button to open the door, then slowly pedaled Magnifico out onto the driveway. His knees practically brushed his ears as his legs rose and fell. He made a grab for the leash and nearly lost his balance.

"Whoa," he muttered as he tried again. The bike wobbled crazily but stayed upright. He rode slowly in a big circle and then up to the fence where Turnip stood watching him with a look of concern on his plain, honest, roman-nosed face.

Alex used his feet to stop the bike and reached a hand through the fence.

Turnip softly lipped his hand and then, having convinced himself that the contraption wasn't about to kill Alex, went back to grazing. Alex rode in a few more big circles, repeating the old words, "dressage, dressage, dressage."

"I must have been the weirdest kid," he muttered

to himself, then promptly fell over when he made another grab for the leash reins.

"You hurt?"

Alex, face burning, tried to stand up but a handlebar was caught on his clothes. When he stood the whole bike came with him. He looked in the direction of the voice as he extracted the handlebar from his pocket and set the bike back on the ground.

"Good thing that little rig's closer to the ground than one of your horses, eh?"

His father sat on the steps of his motor home. Alex wondered how long he'd been there.

Alex rubbed at his scraped knuckles and then felt his bruised elbow. "Yeah," he said.

"You used to ride that damn thing all over hell's half acre," said Mr. Ford. "You were the damndest sight. Making horse noises and talking to yourself like I don't know what. Christ, we had some good laughs about that."

Alex had seen his father only a few times since the confrontation and only from a distance. Something had changed. His father looked different. Thinner. Steadier.

"Are you *sober*?" he asked before he could stop himself.

Mr. Ford looked down at his big hands, which rested on his knees. Then he looked up at Alex.

"I am."

They stayed that way for a moment, Alex holding his childhood bicycle between him and his father.

"That's good, Dad."

Mr. Ford cleared his throat. "I've been going to some meetings. To talk about things. Get a handle on my drinking."

"That's great," said Alex, and he meant it.

"I guess we're going to have to talk about . . . your, your situation, at some point."

Alex stared straight into his father's eyes.

"Do we have to?"

Alex's father gave a short, unexpected bark of laughter.

"A guy just needs a little time," Mr. Ford said, almost as though he was talking to himself. "Does it have anything to do with me living in the RV?" he said suddenly.

"Are you asking if your RV made me gay?"

Alex's father winced. "Not my RV," he said. "Me living in it."

"No, Dad. The fact that you live in a motor home in the yard didn't make me gay. And it isn't

323

because Mom left. Dressage didn't do it to me, either, in case you wondered."

"Bloody hell, this is hard," said Mr. Ford.

"You're telling me," muttered Alex.

All of a sudden Alex was overcome with exhaustion, but strangely, he felt lighter, too, like he'd been packing around a hundred-pound bale of hay and finally just put it down. He noticed his dad slumping a bit on the stairs.

"Well, I think I'm going to head inside. I'm kind of tired," said Mr. Ford.

"Me too," said Alex, slightly too emphatically.

"Talk to you later," said his dad, giving him a little wave.

"Okay," said Alex, waving back.

Alex rolled the bike back to the garage, closed the door, and walked back into the house. On his way through the kitchen he grabbed the phone. He went into his room and shut the door. He sat on his bed and took several deep, calming breaths before he dialed Chris's number.

APRIL 6

Cleo

UNDERGOING A RADICAL personal transformation is no easy thing. Since Tandava colicked and I decided to become a responsible person, I've made a lot of changes. I've been showing up for lessons on time. I've been attending almost all of my classes at school and am on the verge, the very precipice, of catching up. I do almost all of my work around the barn. I still complain quite a bit, but I like to think that's part of my charm. I've also become one of those extremely self-reflective people. Maybe a better way to describe it would be "personally concerned with self."

Since Jenny got kicked out and I got my room all to myself again I've been spending a lot of time writing in my journal. I'm pleased to say that it's no longer a journal of despair. It's more of a journal of self-involvement, really. At least that's what Alex suggested when I read him some of it. He said it in a loving way, though, similar to how he speaks to his sisters and aunt.

On this journey of self-discovery, I've discovered that I have a pattern of giving things away, or rather, letting people take my shit. And my parents' shit.

As Phillipa pointed out, my generous impulses are not the problem. It's the targets and methods of my generosity. I'm choosing unworthy people. Also, there's been a certain underhandedness to my giving. A certain *illegality*, if you will, what with enabling people to break into our house and allowing other people to sell my stuff to get money for drugs.

It occurred to me that there's nothing wrong with helping if you can help the right people the right way.

When Jenny came to pack up her stuff she looked just like she always does. You'd never know that she'd been on a tear for over a week. The only sign that she was in trouble was that she was accompanied by the school's new security guard, Mrs. Mudd's sister, Barb Mudd-Mulvaney, and Ms. Green herself. Mrs. Mudd-Mulvaney is in charge of keeping Stoneleigh students from sneaking out at night. She stood in the doorway making sure that Jenny didn't do anything illegal while she packed up. Ms. Green, who was driving Jenny to the airport, was presumably there for backup.

"Do you mind if I close the door?" Jenny asked. "I've got to get changed."

"We'll be right here," said Ms. Green. "Right outside the door."

Mrs. Mudd-Mulvaney nodded, frowning.

"You do that," said Jenny, swinging the door shut.

"Are you okay?" I asked.

Jenny threw herself onto my bed. "I'm fine. Things just got a little out of hand. Everyone is totally overreacting."

"But you're kicked out."

"So I'm told."

"What did your parents say?"

Jenny slowly closed her eyes. "That's a very good question."

"Didn't you talk to them?"

"Not exactly. I have been informed that I will be flying directly to the finest treatment facility money can buy where my parents will visit me on the very first family day."

"You're going to treatment!" I tried to keep the

awe and horror out of my voice.

"Treatment centers are excellent places to meet celebrities," she said, putting her hands behind her head. "I just hope this place has a pool. The last one didn't. That's probably why I'm not recovered."

"What about Rio?" I asked. "Is she going with you?"

Jenny took a hand out from behind her head and wiped shakily at her nose, betraying, for the first time, that she wasn't completely well. "No. My parents have decided that show jumping is part of the problem. Too many fast people in the jumper world."

"So what are you . . . ?"

"Sell her," Jenny said shortly. "I'm supposed to sell her."

"That's awful," I said.

Jenny sat up suddenly and her hair fell into her face in a fine, blond curtain. She nodded and I thought I heard a sniffle.

The knock on the door made me jump but Jenny didn't react.

"It's time to go, Jennifer. You have a plane to catch," came Ms. Green's voice.

"Is there anything I can do?" I asked.

Jenny pushed her hair to the sides of her face. "Know anyone who wants a nice horse?"

Alex

ALEX LOOKED AT the front door for the fortieth time in ten minutes, willing it to open.

"When is he coming over?" Maggie asked.

"Pardon me?" said Alex, trying to pretend he had no idea what she was talking about.

"Oh please," Maggie said. "You can't fool us. We know you're waiting for Chris."

"What I'm doing is *your* lunch dishes," said Alex.

"You're staring at the door like you're waiting for a million dollars to arrive."

Alex made a dismissive noise and before he could help himself stole another look at the door.

"Don't forget about Fergus's birthday party this afternoon. It's at two o'clock," said Grace as she applied silver polish to her nails at the kitchen table.

"Are we all out now?" May asked Alex, leaning against the counter with a dish towel draped over her shoulder.

"Are we out of what?"

"Out," said May. "If you're out, that makes us out, too."

"Homosexuality is a family affair," said Maggie.

"I'll give you five dollars to never say that again," said Alex.

"We're a gay family now," said May.

"Good for you," said Alex. "But the question is, are we a dishwashing family?"

"Alex, you have to appreciate their efforts to understand your journey as a young, gay man," said Grace.

"Can we please stop talking about this?"

"Chris is your boyfriend," said May in a satisfied voice.

Alex shot yet another look at the doorway.

"We're friends," he said in a low, warning voice. "Me and Chris and Cleo and Sofia. We're all friends."

"I don't think gay people should have to have moustaches," said Maggie.

"What?"

"Wasn't Cleo your moustache? So no one would know you were gay?"

"The term is 'beard,' and no, she wasn't my beard. God."

"High school is such an alienating place for gay, lesbian, bi, and transgendered youth," said May sadly. She always mentioned all the different groups because she wanted to be inclusive.

"You all have to stop talking immediately and bring me your plates."

Five minutes later Chris arrived.

"Hi, Chris." Maggie and May threw open the front door before Alex could take a step away from the sink.

Chris smiled at them and then over at Alex, who had to suppress a huge and ridiculous smile.

"Can we see your drawings again?" asked Maggie and May. Chris brought his square black sketchbook over to the table and opened it.

"That's so cool!" said May.

"That's us!" said Maggie, as though she hadn't already seen the drawing of her and her sister a dozen times.

Finally Grace intervened. "Okay, you two. Go get

in the car. I'll drop you off at practice on my way."

She turned to Alex and Chris. "I'm off to do Vanessa Pringle's hair."

"Coach Pringle? From Stoneleigh?" said Alex. "I would have guessed that she cut her hair with horse clippers."

"I think she does. That's why I'm stepping in. Anyway, I'll see you at Fergus and Ivan's later."

Alex and Chris nodded.

When the room was finally quiet, Alex turned to Chris. "You want to go for a walk?"

They walked along the road and turned up toward Ms. Reed's. Since they'd begun spending time together, they'd gone for many walks and almost every one ended up there. On their walks Chris talked about applying to art school and about the music he was working on, about bands that excited him. Alex was pleased he was able to nod knowingly, thanks to his research on the Internet. Alex talked about what dressage had meant to him, what horses meant to him. About how much he missed riding dressage.

When they reached the edge of the fence line, Alex whistled and Detroit, who'd been standing at the far corner of the pasture, lifted his head and whinnied. Alex whistled again and Detroit trotted toward them and then broke into a canter.

When he skidded to a stop at the fence, Alex grinned and rubbed the horse's black-tipped nose and scratched his ears.

Chris reached over and patted Detroit's neck under his mane.

Then he reached into his messenger bag and pulled out his sketchbook.

"I have something to show you," he said. "I came by here the other day. By myself."

Chris flipped open his sketchbook to the last page.

Alex saw that Chris had drawn Detroit, standing, just like he was now, with his head over the fence, his ears pricked with interest, his mane tangled in the breeze.

"I know you miss him so I wanted to give you this. I don't know. It's something, anyway," said Chris.

Alex couldn't speak for a moment, so he just nodded and bit his lip.

The two boys stood in the shade of a big maple tree at the corner of the paddock. They stood shoulder to shoulder. Alex reached over and took Chris's hand in his. Without thinking about it or turning to see if anyone was watching, Alex leaned over and kissed him. They kissed until Detroit started snuffling their hair and broke it up.

The driveway was full of cars when Chris and Alex arrived at the party.

"Hasn't taken Fergus long to make friends," said Alex, thinking ruefully that it had taken him almost seventeen years to make four.

"You're here!" said Cleo, coming out of the barn to give each of them a hug. "You will be disgusted to learn that I *bicycled* over here," she said. She raised one of her legs to show off the thick, white tights she wore under her kilt.

"Aren't they revolting!" she said. "But I had no choice. They're being very strict right now about keeping us in our uniforms when we go out in public."

Alex noticed that the right leg of the tights was ripped and covered in grease.

"Did you wipe out?"

"Totally! I'm even worse on a bike than I was in a car. Somehow I got my tights caught in the chain of that piece of crap. I can't believe that's the best transportation the school can provide. Considering how much tuition we pay. Lance Armstrong probably couldn't ride that bike. But I'm helping Phillipa to get in shape and part of that means riding bikes."

"And part of it is you losing your license," said Phillipa, coming up behind Cleo.

"Oh, that," said Cleo.

"Okay, we should head down to the house," Alex said.

The party was nice enough and it was good to be surrounded by people he knew and liked, but he couldn't shake the left-out feeling that came over him whenever he spent any time at Limestone Farm. He wanted to talk about dressage but to do so made him heartsick. Plus, he had the uncomfortable feeling that everyone wanted him to leave. Maybe they felt bad for him. Finally he took the hint and asked Chris to drive him home. Then he was offended when Chris acted like he couldn't get rid of him fast enough. Chris practically pushed him out of the car after making some feeble excuse about having to get home for dinner.

After Alex had recovered from the indignity of being dumped off so unceremoniously, he noticed a hole in the yard where his father's motor home used to be. His heart sank. Had his father run off, unable to cope with sobriety, not to mention his gay son? Was he driving drunk around the streets of Nanaimo in a giant recreational vehicle? Alex's stomach cramped at the thought.

He ran into the house and called but got no answer. He walked quickly out to the barn. As he was opening the gate, his father appeared in the doorway of the barn.

"Where's the RV?"

"Sold it," said his father shortly.

What was going on?

"Is everything all right?"

"It's fine. There's something in the barn. Something I want you to see."

That sounded ominous. Maybe his father had found a real cowboy to be his son, a rough-and-ready guy who liked big-haired cowgirls. A son his dad could brag about down at the pub. Maybe the new son was waiting in the barn to bash Alex over the head and hide his body in the manure pile.

"Just come have a look."

Alex walked slowly into the barn. The first thing he saw was a refined head poking over the second stall door. Alex looked back at his father.

"There's a horse in there," said Alex, realizing as he said it that it wasn't the sharpest comment he'd ever made.

"That's right."

"Whose . . . ?"

"Yours," said Mr. Ford.

Alex tried to take in what his father was saying.

"Where'd it come from?"

"Her. It's a mare. Your friend Cleo told me about her. I guess some girl at that school of hers had to leave it behind."

Alex looked carefully at the horse. "Is this *Jenny's* horse? Rio?"

"That's right. That's her name," said his father.

"But she's a top jumper."

"Should be for what I paid for her. You can use her for your dressage. That lady coach up there at the school said she's real athletic."

Alex walked over to take a closer look. The mare was nearly as tall as Detroit had been. Her coat shone coppery red over her muscles.

He looked back at his father as a thought came to him. "Is this why you sold your motor home?"

"This, and I had to get the business straightened out."

Alex glanced back at Rio. Good jumpers were expensive and Rio was a great jumper.

"Plus, I thought it was time I moved back into the house," added Mr. Ford.

Alex glanced at Rio again. It was like his eyes were adjusting to the sun. The red mare got more beautiful every time he looked at her.

At that moment May came barreling into the barn. "Is it over?" she gasped.

"Did we miss it?" asked Maggie, who was right behind her.

"What?" asked Alex and Mr. Ford.

"Only the most touching family moment ever," said May. "Where the depressed boy gets his dream horse!"

"Now will you let us use Turnip as a stunt horse?" said Maggie.

Grace, who'd come in and was leaning against the doorway near her brother, crossed her arms over her chest. "See, shit like this is why I'm reluctant to get my own place," she said.

Mr. Ford came back into the barn later that night as Alex was putting Rio away. Alex had given the mare a thorough brushing and spent some time getting to know her. She had a quick intelligence in her eyes that he liked very much. Dressage uses different muscles than jumping and requires a different mind-set, but working with her was a task he looked forward to.

"So, you think she'll work out for you?" Mr. Ford said.

Alex let himself out of Rio's stall and slid the latch shut. Then he gave Turnip, who'd been watching the goings-on with great interest, a scratch behind the ears.

"She's a beautiful horse," he said. "We'll just have to see if she likes dressage."

"If anyone can bring her around, I figure you can. You've always been real good with horses."

Alex nodded while staring at the floor. He felt uncomfortably full of emotion. He didn't want to do something dumb like cry, so he bit his lip.

"It's like Rudy Chapman down at the Wheat Sheaf used to say. Just ride her straight."

Alex shot his dad a wry look and Mr. Ford blushed.

"Well, you know what I mean."

Alex nodded. He knew exactly what his dad meant.

"Anyway, your friend Cleo's here. She's with the girls right now. I told her I'd let you know she was here."

"Okay, thanks, Dad."

Alex watched his father walk away and then he looked back at the two horses staring at him over their stall doors. For a moment he was afraid to move. Afraid that it was all too good to be true. Afraid that if he took a wrong step it would all come crashing down.

"Practicing your statue impersonation?" asked Cleo as she walked into the barn.

Alex turned and gave her a small smile. "Nah, just looking. She's amazing, Cleo."

"I know. I'm glad she's got a good home. What am I saying? She's landed in the best home in the world."

"I just wanted to say thank you. I know this was your doing."

"I just planted the seed. Then I watered it and gave it sunlight. That's all."

Alex laughed and Cleo's small face lit up with pleasure.

"Are you coming in? You promised you'd watch videos with me."

"Okay. I'll be right there."

"I should warn you that there are no horses in these videos. No dressage."

"That's fine."

"What they do have is Owen Wilson."

"That's more than fine, then."

Alex turned out the hall light and took a final glance at his horses. Then he turned and followed Cleo out of the barn.

ACKNOWLEDGMENTS

THIS BOOK WOULDN'T have been possible without generous help and advice of the following people:

Paul Forster, whose advice and encouragement were essential; Stephanie Dubinsky for her insights and cheerleading; Meg Cabot for encouragement and excellent suggestions; Deborah Fox of Foxborough Farms, a fine horsewoman and dressage coach, who helped in a hundred ways; Jennifer Brownlow for sharing her extensive knowledge of horses and the sport of dressage; Mike McGuire and Angela Quek for allowing me to lease Mike's horse, a gentle giant called Edward the Grey. Ed rekindled my love of riding, and Mike and Angela reminded me of all that is wonderful about horse people; Selena Pellizzari, who read an early draft of the book and whose riding abilities continue to inspire me; Elena, Leigh, Annette, and Lucy Bonar, who took such wonderful care of my horse, Tango, and read early drafts of this book; Robyn King who runs Cedar Creek Farms, where Tango currently and very happily resides, as well as Colleen Purcell, Pam Williams, and Rose Locke, my fellow boarders, all of whom "test rode" the manuscript. I'd like to thank Susan Harrison at Queen Margaret's School, who allowed me to take a tour of their riding facilities. I must point out here that although seeing Queen Margaret's gave me the idea to set part of the novel in a girl's equestrian school, the fact that both are girls' equestrian private schools on Vancouver Island is where the resemblance ends. QMS, as it is known, is one of the finest schools in British Columbia and a source of much pride in the Canadian equestrian and educational communities. Stoneleigh, my fictional school, and its denizens are entirely a product of my fevered imagination.

I'd also like to thank the usual heroes: Bill Juby, who read the manuscript approximately four hundred times without complaint; Wendy Banta for pep talks and votes of confidence; Marjorie Phillips for welcome opinions; Diane McIntosh for her unique genius; my agent, Hilary, for everything; Lynne Missen for her encouragement and input; and, of course, Ruth Katcher, my editor, who didn't throw up her hands in despair but instead pushed me to get it right.

I'd also like to thank my early riding instructors and mentors and last, but not least, I want to express my gratitude to all the horses who have put up with me over the years. I will never cease to be amazed by the generosity of spirit, grace, and dignity that are the hallmarks of the horse.